WITHDRAWN

REPAIR MY HOUSE

Repair My House

by

Glen Williamson

Creation House

Carol Stream, Illinois

REPAIR MY HOUSE © 1973 by Creation House. All rights reserved. Printed in the United States of America. No part of this book may be reproduced in any manner whatsoever without written permission except in the case of brief quotations embodied in reviews. For information, address Creation House, 499 Gundersen Drive, Carol Stream, Illinois 60187.

Library of Congress Catalog Card Number: 73-81984
International Standard Book Number: 0-88419-042-0

To four lovely ladies, the *Franciscan Sisters of the Atonement,* who welcomed a Protestant minister and his wife to their guest house in Assisi, and gave valuable assistance in the production of this work.

Contents

Foreword

History records that God has His chosen man or men, institution or organizations, for every generation. The history of revival shows that dedicated men have been raised up across the centuries to present the claims of John 3:16, "For God so loved the world, that He gave His only begotten Son, that whoever believes in Him should not perish, but have eternal life." Francis of Assisi was one of those chosen vessels fully yielded to God's will as well as being committed to follow the disciplines of such a commitment. Francis was one who both planted and reaped revival harvest. Here is the story of an authentic, transparent New Testament Christian.

In the quiet town of Assisi, in the Province of Perugia, 1,345 feet above sea level, with a lovely view of the vale of Spoletti, St. Francis was born in 1182 and in this same town, died in 1226. In his day, already a boy of recognized leadership among other youth, no one would have suspicioned that he would become the founder of the Franciscans and furthermore, would be canonized in 1228. This man of meager education, even in his day, had within him a sense of destiny. He was tender-hearted and a man possessing a genuine spirit of charity. Even though he was born into a family of means, he had only sympathy for the poor, especially the lepers. Yet the heart of Francis yearned for an inner peace, a peace which he knew he could not purchase with money.

Francis' youthful years were distraught over the inequities experienced by people in civil government as well as inconsistencies of the church expressed by everyday living not in harmony with its teachings. He and his best friend decided that they could not change the church nor the civil government by revolution; only a spiritual awakening within the church would revolutionize society.

As he looked over the Tiber Valley and down into the streets of Assisi from the roof of his father's home, he felt the call of God. In fact, he indicates that he saw a vision which resolved itself in the call of God to preach to the poor in Assisi. It seemed that Matthew 10:7-9 confirmed his call.

And as ye go, preach, saying, "The kingdom of heaven is at hand." Heal the sick, raise the dead, cleanse the lepers, cast out demons; freely you received, freely give. Do not acquire gold, or silver, or copper for your money belts.

In 1209, he began to preach. Disciples joined him. When they became twelve in number he obtained the sanction of Innocent III to form an order of the church. They each then gave themselves to apostolic preaching and work among the poor.

He was a most lovable man possessing a personality of strong contrasts. These were exemplified by tenderness and compassion coupled with versatile dynamic action. Yet this many-faceted personality was completely embued with the desire to genuinely imitate Christ. In spite of two serious illnesses he constantly manifested a joyful spirit. He was self-disciplined and endowed with a spirit of prayer.

The life of Francis has been examined by the theological world, both Catholic and Protestant, and volumes have been written. This volume, however, can be read and understood with very little or no background understanding of the life of Francis. The book comes as a volume geared to the nontheological person with the purpose of portraying character qualities that could well be emulated today. Its factual base, put in fictional form, is most exciting reading.

The author portrays Francis well, largely because he himself has an appreciation of aesthetics that enables him to sense and interpret the spirit of Francis. His spirit literally breathes in the pages of this book.

One should read through this volume in one sitting. I am sure that anyone starting the book will want to do so.

Repair My House should have a wide reading by both Protestants and Catholics. It could be that this will be one of the books that will inspire ministers and laymen of this day to pay the price for revival as did Francis.

Dr. Paul P. Petticord

Preface

For a number of years I knew about as much—or as little—of the life and ministry of Saint Francis of Assisi as do most other Protestants. I was aware that he was a small barefoot man, wedded to poverty; he wrote prayers and poems, loved animals, and preached to the birds. Then, some years ago, I entered into a systematic study of the revivals of the church and began to see a half-hidden star in the thirteenth-century sky. That star appeared to be trying hard to break through the literary smog—a mixture of fairy tales and truth—that surrounded the little friar whom God had called to "repair His house." My interest began to grow—for months I poured over every biography of Francis, old and new, that became available to me, until I felt that I knew the little saint as well as I know any of my contemporaries. His appearance, his ambitions, his humility, his reactions to success and failure, and his utter fearlessness of life and death—the whole spectrum of his personality—became so real to me that, later, when I walked the streets of Assisi doing research, it seemed sometimes that I might meet the little evangelist just around the next corner.

It soon became evident to me that one thing the world did not need was another biography of Francis—a further attempt to dig out and document the facts of his life and work. This had been done in the most scholarly fashion by learned men who spent their lives at the task. Instead I sensed the need for a work that would tell his remarkable story in the language of Protestant laymen.

There was one problem. The early writers, contemporaries of Francis, who could have given details necessary to support the amazing facts of this life, failed apparently to see the need of doing it. For instance, we are told that Francis' first disciple was a fabulously rich nobleman named Bernard di Quintavalle, who, immediately following his conversion, gave away every penny of his fortune, dressed himself in sackcloth, and lived in abject poverty the rest of his life. Standing alone, this bit of data might be accepted by the average mind as fiction, but never as fact. There were circumstances, of course, that made the story plausible enough to the early writers, but would modern readers believe it? In *Repair My House,* details, incidents, and when necessary even characters—tailor-made to fit the circumstances—have been added to fill in the gaps.

Although this work is definitely an historical *novel,* I have taken great care to neither distort nor delete any clearly documented facts. Where there is controversy, the position which seems most realistic to me has been adopted. So, while most biographers agree that Francis had an older brother named Angelo, and others say that Francis was an only son, I took the latter position because it seems the more likely. And I have made Angelo a relative, rather than a son, of Francis' father.

The writings of many authors, of course, were carefully considered in preparation for this work, but none are quoted—hence, the absence of footnotes and bibliography.

Introduction

Tourists in Italy, flying hurriedly from Naples to Rome to Florence, often miss her villages and lovely, rolling countryside. Blessed is the man who remains at home to read geography and watch travelogues if, in his journeyings, he is unable to escape the world's established tourist lanes.

To the north of Rome, a hundred miles or so, between Perugia and Foligno, the ancient city of Assisi gazes down upon the vale of Umbria. Its lazy rivers and silent glades have never failed to inspire both artists and poets to their best endeavors. It was here that Perugino practiced long with oils and canvas. The tourist who is fortunate enough to spend a day or two in Assisi sees Italy not only as it is but as it was. To the casual ear and eye, the flutter of tiny automobiles and a few up-to-date buildings mark the only changes of importance the centuries have wrought.

A portly woman with a shopping bag on her arm visits

15

with a friend exactly as her mother did thirty years ago. Three hundred years earlier another ancestor gossiped with a neighbor beside the same cobblestone thoroughfare. And since this is an ancient community, such mouth-to-mouth resuscitation of long forgotten transgressions, together with choice morsels of real news, was common in Assisi many centuries before that.

So it happened that one morning in June, a full three hundred years before Italy's Christopher Columbus discovered a new world, just such a conversation was taking place before a market in Assisi. The two women were overly excited—a situation not uncommon in that part of the world—as they discussed an important wedding that had been announced by the parish priest the evening before.

It seemed that a certain wealthy townsman, Pietro di Bernardone, a dealer in cloth, whose frequent and lengthy visits to the great cities had gained him a cloudy reputation, had won the hand of the petite and lovely lady, Pica, who had come from France.

"That Pietro always gets just what he wants!" One of the women was fairly screaming to her friend.

"Dear Pica," the other responded, "she can use his money and that is all. Tragedy will come! She'll move into his big house and raise him a family, spending long hours alone while he goes carrying on in Rome and Athens. And since she can't really love him, she will lavish her love upon his children, and what a spoiled bunch of young ones that will be!"

Pietro and Pica were married, and the ensuing years proved that the screaming gossips had not been very far off in their prophecies. Pica bore a son for the meandering Pietro (he was in Paris at the time). She christened the boy Giovanni, then nicknamed him Francesco. She tried in vain to spoil him, being convinced that he was destined for greatness.

Francis, as the boy was called, began soon to favor his mother in appearance. Slight of stature, sensitive of nature, with delicate features framed in an oval face, sharp black eyes, thick black hair, and a bubbling sense of humor, he became a marked individualist. As a lad he was the most personable boy in town. He liked people, a characteristic that far outweighed the fact that he wasn't as pretty as some of his little friends.

Through preadolescence Francis was an imaginative lad—always leader of a gang that went romping through the streets, scrambling up great stone stairways and over moldy walls, later to meet in some secluded spot to plan further and more dangerous escapades. When they played school, Francis was the teacher. When their game involved robbers rushing a feudal castle perched atop its protective hill, Francis was always the baron. With a few wisely chosen fellows of superior strength and daring, he fought off the invading hordes. And occasionally, of course, their play became a bit destructive—especially when a dozen or more shouting lance-bearing lads running at top speed would follow the bright-eyed Francis through the stalls of the market.

Irate citizens, in bands of twos and threes, were constantly confronting Pica with exaggerated stories of the escapades of the juveniles, of which they always said her boy was responsible. She listened with smiling eyes and paid, without a word, whatever damages were presented. Then, forgetting to scold the guilty culprits, she would invite them into the tiny courtyard back of her great residence to reward them with all the goodies of her pantry. She called them all her sons.

Once, when Francis was sternly accused by a merchant whose fruit stand had been raided, the indulgent mother paid the bill and stated firmly that she doubted Francis' guilt, and anyway no real harm was done. Later, though, when Francis came home hungry and tired from his play, she decided to question him as she fixed a late afternoon snack.

"Francis," she began, "did you really take fruit from old Gilberto's stand? And why? Your father provides all the money you ever need."

"I didn't steal anything, Mother," he answered. "It was Andrea, but don't tell anyone. His father is poor and Andrea never has any money. Yesterday I bought him an apple. That's why he went home crying today when Gilberto accused me of the stealing. He'll be all right. Tomorrow I will buy him another apple."

Then Pica and Francis laughed together as they sat enjoying their figs and cheese cake.

Pica never doubted her son's veracity and certainly not his future. On one occasion, with a simple, direct statement, she dismissed two nosy neighbors who made disparaging remarks about his "ever growing up to amount to anything."

"I am sure," she said with conviction, "that if it please God, he will become a good Christian."

How prophetic her statement was she had no way of knowing. But we know, of course, that this carefree boy was to be one of the few favored figures in history upon whom God would lay His hand for sweeping revival.

Francis found it easy to love his mother.

Pietro di Bernardone was a selfish, overbearing man of business and a seeker after pleasure. Pica was well aware that his reckless exploits in both areas were so questionable as to raise the eyebrows of all who knew him, but he was her husband, the father of her child, and an excellent provider. Many women of her acquaintance had it worse—much, much worse.

On his return trips to Assisi, Pietro would labor diligently to catch up the work at his elaborate drygoods counter, which was located in the large lower front room of the Bernardone residence. To the townspeople he was a shrewd and grasping merchant, relentless as steel. But to Francis he was an overly indulgent parent, taking great pleasure in bringing home expensive gifts—including the latest in fashionable attire. In return for these extravagances Pietro expected loyalty, love, and devotion, but he was more than vaguely aware that these unpurchasable commodities were never freely forthcoming.

Francis, to be brutally frank, did not trust his father. He appreciated the gifts, enjoyed the security of the home, and reveled secretly sometimes in Pietro's boasting of him to the customers in the shop. Still there was a marked absence of the closeness that should have characterized a father-son relationship as congenial as this one appeared to be.

Even so, the father was more than a little pleased as he watched his son, dressed in togs the others could not afford, exercise leadership over his playmates. He secretly enjoyed the little disturbances caused by the boys even when petty larceny and minor acts of vandalism were involved.

He had great plans, of course, for Francis to take over his lucrative business by-and-by. He lost no opportunity to train him, carefully explaining the many tricks of the trade.

Francis cared nothing for the art of making money. Why should he? From his earliest recollections he had never known the need for it. And even if he were to pursue a business career, he had no interest in the silks and linens of his father's store. He thought that he might raise horses or breed dogs.

Francis would have made a good actor. His pretended interest in his father's business was so well executed that the ambitious parent never doubted his son's sincerity.

"Look at this purple cloth," Pietro said one day when the two were alone behind the counter. "It is very common in France and most *inexpensive.*" Then, with a knowing wink he lowered his voice and continued, "But many people in a town like this, expecially the women; they think it is exquisite and are willing to scrimp and save to pay a high price for it. Remember that when you are waiting on customers in my absence."

Then, playfully slapping the boy on the shoulder—assuming that he was bursting with pride for being considered old enough to share so important a secret—the father continued blindly.

"One day, when you are older, I will take you with me on one of my trips. We will have great fun together." Then, throwing all caution to the wind, he nudged the boy in the ribs and hinted of some of the amusements and pleasures to which he would introduce his son when they were far from family, friends, and the gossiping tongues of Assisi.

Francis, who had just turned twelve, was shocked with horror at his father's carnal suggestions. Biting his lip in an effort to curb his feelings, he broke away and ran through the house to the courtyard where Pica was quietly resting in her favorite chair. To her amazement, he threw his arms

19

around her and wept hard and long, sobbing profusely. Pica never discovered the reason for his outbreak.

What, Francis wondered, *would be his father's reaction if suddenly he were to displease him?* He recoiled at the thought of it. Nowhere in the boy's make-up, really, could be found a disposition to hate anyone. It troubled him to know that his own father, who treated him like a prince, came closer to stirring within him this despicable emotion than anyone he knew.

Then came the day for Pietro to pack his bag for another journey. As always, the good-byes were said with Pica weeping and Francis, pretending sorrow, telling his father to return sooner .next time, knowing full well that home would be a much more congenial place for his mother and him as soon as Pietro had departed.

Francis found it hard to love his father.

1

The Naked King

Among the boys of Assisi was Gallo, a tall, thin lad with sallow cheeks and large pale blue eyes. At seventeen he was an ardent student, strongly opinionated, and already branded a heretic. Gallo was something of a recluse; he was a revolutionary, fanatically religious, with a compelling passion for change. He was wise enough to know that the seeds of reformation take root most easily in the pliable minds of preadolescents. His was a long-range plan.

His greatest delight was to gather the boys of Francis' gang into a circle in an effort to mold their thinking by telling dramatic and tragic tales he had gleaned from his reading.

"Let me tell you the story of the *naked king*," he began one afternoon.

"Naked king?" they echoed. "Hey, that sounds better

than anything you've told us yet! Wait, here comes Francis! We want him to hear it too."

When the boys were seated about their leader, the fluent Gallo began to spin his historical yarn. It involved King Henry IV of Germany who, in 1077, had dared to defy Pope Gregory. Later, in serious trouble and seeking reconciliation, the king crossed the mountains to appear outside the castle of Canossa where the Pope was staying. Here his majesty was forced to wait barefooted and nearly naked for three nights in the raw January weather before the haughty Gregory would give him audience. It was a morbid story, excellently told.

Gallo continued, swiftly approaching his climax. "The whole picture is as devastating as the leprosy," he cried. "This act of torture, done in the name of Christ and His church, is only one of a thousand events that should have warned the people long ago that the church is corrupt, apostate, and has outlived the usefulness for which she was created!"

Gallo was either a brave or reckless lad, for these were dangerous words. It was well that his audience was made up of boys from ten to fourteen, who only partially understood him, and who couldn't do much about it anyway.

Francis, alone, appeared to be unimpressed even though the turmoil of the times was not easy for him or for anyone else to understand. All Europe was plagued with insecurity and unrest. Russia had long been fighting the savage Mongols and Tartars; the Moors, having crossed from Africa, were terrorizing Spain; Frederick I (Red Beard), avowed enemy of papal absolutism, was on the German throne, and Britain was torn by civil war.

Italy fared worse. The Roman Empire was breathing her last, and feudal barons, from their stark medieval castles, were waging wars upon one another. The Crusades were at the midway point of their inglorious history, and the church, seriously divided, had reached its darkest hour as a spiritual force in the world. Ironically, the church, at the same time, had become a political giant; the popes were wielding power, unprecedented in history, with many of the church's strongest critics under their sway.

Even the town of Assisi was notorious for its looseness of morals. The Parish Church of Saint Nicholas, where Francis and his mother faithfully attended mass, was the scene of unbelievable debauchery each year from the sixth of December (that saint's feast day when a boy bishop was installed) until Christmas. The whole moral tone was so low that the era became known in history as *Pornocracy* or *The Reign of Harlots*. It was all very confusing to open-minded young people.

Gallo was not unique as a young dissenter. Many Italian youth, confused and disillusioned, were no longer willing to accept the mandates of their elders who had failed miserably to establish any kind of peace and security in the world. Every able-bodied boy knew that one day soon he would be marching off to battle, and no one was sure for whom or what he would be fighting.

Gallo's eyes were fixed upon Francis. "It is our generation only that can change the world." he stated boldly. "It is our generation that must produce a leader who has the courage, strength, and intelligence to accomplish the inevitable!" The youthful storyteller finished in a burst of oratory.

A few moments later Gallo quietly approached Francis with an important proposition. "Bernardone," he said, in an effort to impress the boy, "you have unusual leadership qualities. If you will join me, we shall see a movement started that some day may sweep the world. And who knows, you may be the one to head it up!"

"No, Gallo," said Francis, forcing a smile, "it isn't God that's wrong. It's the people. Oh, I expect to be a great leader some day, perhaps a general or a knight, but I am not your man. You will have to find another." He smiled again, but a wistful expression crept into his deep, black eyes that hinted of a seriousness hidden somewhere far beneath the surface in his strange personality.

Francis was disturbed even though an ugly, century-old indignity toward an enemy ruler should not have triggered his emotions. To his sensitive soul the story of the naked king was a symbol of all that is unpretty in an otherwise delightful, wonderful world.

At home he made his way slowly up a stairway to a favorite lookout on the rooftop. There, in an effort to dispel the depression that enveloped his spirit, he lay on a rug, his slender hands cupped beneath his chin, and gazed across the city. Its substantial dwellings of stone and wood built upon the mountain's upward slope always intrigued the imaginative Francis. Each edifice, colorful and magnificent, appeared to be standing on its tiptoes peering over the head of the one before it. Suddenly the boy's depression lifted, leaving in its wake an ecstasy that flooded his soul and blinded his eyes with tears of gladness, so that for one long moment, he felt that he loved the whole world enough even to die for it.

Then, in the distance, Francis caught sight of a leper signaling his uncleanness and begging for alms. The moment of ecstasy vanished. It would not be fair to say that Francis despised the lepers, but it was true that he found them altogether repulsive to his sensitive nature. Whenever he met one of the wretched souls, he would close his eyes, hold his nose, and run past on the windward side to avoid sight of the grotesque features and the stench of the open sores.

Just now, as he dwelt upon these things, his thoughts condemned him. He was sorry; but he knew that he was not sorry enough to effect any particular change in his reactions the next time he would meet a leper. He was ashamed and longed for peace. Francis had never been a particularly religious lad, but in the sanctuary of this emotion-packed moment—clutching a miniature crucifix—he believed without reservation that Christ, the Author of peace, was more important than anyone or anything upon Earth. And he found himself longing intensely for the approving smile of the Man of Sorrows.

Everything he could see from the vantage point of his own rooftop was beautiful to behold. It was that which he could not see that continued to disturb his sensitive soul. Well he knew that far below the tops of those noble dwellings, opening into filthy alleys were tiny, vermin-infested rooms that housed Assisi's poor, And while his friends were

24

unaware of it, Francis knew that in one of those rooms, some-where in the maze of narrow streets and alleys, lived the crusading Gallo with his invalid mother.

In those hovels—located at the base of mansions—hunger, disease, and fear were omnipresent. There the ragged children limited their area of play to the garbage-strewn alleys, fearful of the sons of more affluent citizens who monopolized the streets and fearlessly stormed the market-place. Only a dreamer like Gallo possessed the motivation necessary to wash his body, brush his clothes, and improve his mind that he might come up from the alleys to invade a culture so far removed from that in which he lived.

Most of the boys of Francis' gang were openly cynical toward the riffraff that huddled in the unlovely darkness of Assisi's slums. They were aware that in those gloomy, smelly rooms, the horrid leprosy was bred and born. Out from their din and squalor came one and then another and another whose scaly sores condemned them to lives of awful tor-ture beyond the city's wall. They knew also that the dread disease was no respecter of persons, and upon occasion a son of noble birth could be stricken with the malady.

In his meditation Francis recalled with a start that once he had seen such a one—leaving home and friends forever staggering down a great stone stairway, weeping and wailing like a lost soul on the brink of perdition. Whenever the in-cident was brought to mind, he shuddered with horror and sometimes heard the despairing cries again in his dreams.

So it was that Francis decided to see the bishop, his father confessor. He would have talked with Pica, but he knew his adoring mother could not possibly understand his prob-lem. To her, the security provided by her husband, by the love of her son, and by a vague notion that heaven awaited those who walked according to the tenets of the church was everything she needed to make life a most worthwhile experiment.

On his way out Francis paused on the patio to tell Pica, who was reclining again in her favorite chair, that he was going to the church. She smiled her approval, completely oblivious of the turmoil that raged within his breast. After all, he was *merely* a twelve-year-old boy.

Bishop Guido was out when Francis arrived at the

church. However, the boy was welcomed informally by an associate priest, the amiable Father Joseph, who was forever spreading sunshine and laughing with the people. He was everybody's friend. To him lightness and levity were the perfect tools with which to pry loose any heaviness of heart and soul. But with these tools Francis had long been wonderfully endowed, laughing his way out of every difficulty. Today, to the earnest lad who faced the priest, any lightness, levity, or laughter could be nothing less than sacrilegious, as he bared his soul. "I think," he concluded, "that God wants me for some special work, and I am not yet worthy even to be called His son." He was the picture of despair.

The priest smiled broadly; to erase that picture was his only burden. After all —he reasoned as Pica had done—he was dealing merely with a twelve-year-old boy.

"Why, Francis," he said, "if I recall correctly, your grades at school are in the lower bracket, and your reputation about town is a bit cloudy sometimes. Didn't I hear of you taking fruit from old Gilberto's stand recently? Now don't think that I'm scolding—I was a boy once, too, you know. But can't you see how silly are these notions that disturb your childish mind? Come now, give your old friend a real big smile; then run, play with the boys." Then, with a hearty laugh, he slapped the lad on the shoulder and closed the little session saying, "Everything will be all right."

Father Joseph was not the counselor that Francis needed. Deeply hurt, the boy ran out into the street, past the market, and into the country. He dropped down, nearly winded, at the foot of a giant tree—a favorite spot overlooking the vale of Umbria—and gave full vent to his emotions. He cried until there seemed to be no more tears to come. Then after making his way down to a brook, he washed his face and started homeward, a boy altogether unhappy and confused.

Francis found it hard to forget the story of the naked king.

2

Stormy Teens

On his way back into town Francis passed the home of Bernard di Quintavalle, a successful young bachelor, who like Francis' father, Pietro, sometimes made trips to the great markets. Some days before, the paths of the two merchants had crossed; so together they traveled home to Assisi, arriving while Francis was sitting beneath his favorite tree in the country. To the boy's unbounded delight, a beautiful black filly, the finest bit of horseflesh he had ever seen was tethered outside the Quintavalle residence. Forgetting his spiritual problem, Francis quickly approached the animal, talking to her in a soothing, loving voice. He was rewarded with a low whinnying response. The boy put his arm around the shiny black neck, ran his fingers through the soft mane, and patted the filly's nose with tenderness, as only an animal lover like himself would dare to do.

"It looks as though you two have struck up an early

acquaintance," said Bernard Quintevalle as he came around the corner of the portico. "I am glad you like her. You can guess that she cost a lot of money."

"Oh, sir! May I buy her? May I? I'll give you almost all my allowance every month for a year—two years. I'll work for you! I'll do anything! Please, may I have her?" Francis was so intense that Bernard didn't dare to smile.

"She isn't mine to sell. I'm sorry," said the man. "Why don't you run home and talk to your father? Maybe he can help you."

The boy started to leave, then stopped to face the youthful merchant again. "Thank you, sir," he said fervently. "Oh, thank you, sir."

"Good luck, Francis." Bernard was smiling broadly now.

Francis ran the short distance to his home where he was met by his proud, indulgent parents. He always looked forward to the gifts his father brought from the city, but this time he was too excited to care. Hardly pausing to greet his father, whom he hadn't seen for weeks, he began telling about the beautiful black filly.

"May I have her?" he cried. "I'll give up my allowance! I'll work at the counter for nothing! I'll do anything if only I can have her!" Pietro and Pica had never seen him so excited before.

"Now just a minute, Son," Pietro was enjoying himself immensely. "No, you can't buy her; she is already purchased and paid for. I took care of that. Nor can you earn her; you will receive wages for your work. The filly you saw tethered at Bernard's house was supposed to be a surprise. She is my gift to you, but you must make preparation to receive her."

"What do you mean?" Francis cried, almost beside himself with joy.

"You must build a stall and manger with your own hands." There was no doubting that Pietro meant exactly what he was saying nor that Francis would be started with his task that very hour.

Doing the work of a carpenter was not easy for a twelve-year-old boy, but diligent indeed were the efforts extended. After two hard days the stall and manger were completed to Pietro's satisfaction, and Francis ran to get his prize.

The extravagant Pietro had also purchased a leather saddle and bridle, imports from Britain, where harness making was bcoming a recognized trade. There was a riding suit, too. Francis rode proudly up and down the streets of Assisi, the envy of every boy who saw him.

Pica was proud also, for she saw that Francis was allowing the poorer boys to ride. "My son doesn't have one conceited hair in his head," she told a neighbor. And this was probably only a minor exaggeration.

In the months that followed, important events piled up swiftly for Francis. Pending warfare between Assisi and her neighboring city, Perugia, was common talk, and Francis, whose voice was changing (puberty comes earlier in Italy than in some parts of the world) began visualizing himself a man, a soldier, a hero, perhaps even a *knight*. He discovered rather suddenly, too, that the girls of Assisi were becoming attractive to him, and when a band of troubadors from Paris appeared on the streets, he was deeply engrossed.

It was on rare occasions now that he thought about the spiritual struggle he had undergone a few months earlier. He spoke to no one about it; but neither did he discount its importance nor deny its reality. Rather, he buried his more serious thoughts in the rolling sea of revelry in which he was fast assuming leadership of Assisi's teen-age society, even if he was the youngest of the lot. It should be said in Francis' favor, though, that temperance in all things was the rule of his life and he was always discreet with women.

When Francis was sixteen, a new pope, who took the name of Innocent III, ascended the pontifical throne. His iron hand liberated Assisi and many of her sister cities from the rule of feudal lords. It was a great day as the Assisian men stormed the castle that long had stared menacingly down upon them, burned everything that was flammable, and before they were through, nearly ruined the city with more than a score of fires. The Perugians looked on with great delight.

When it was over, the work of reconstruction began. Francis assisted the laborers by carrying stone, mixing mortar, and laying blocks and bricks until he became proficient at the mason's trade. He had never really worked before and discovered that he liked it. It satisfied a half-starved creative instinct and made him feel useful in a world that theretofore had been mostly pleasure.

The rebuilt city—a work well done—gave its sons a certain sense of pride, and a new patriotism burned within their hearts. They bragged that someday, in the not too distant future, they would storm Perugia and burn her to the ground. However, two more peaceful years slipped by, and Francis, still a beardless youth, reached his eighteenth birthday.

He was riding along a road at the edge of the city one afternoon when he came upon what he thought was an elderly man trudging slowly with a cane. For a moment he feared the man was a leper, but no signal of uncleanness was forthcoming. Francis pulled up his mount and looked squarely into the poor fellow's face. To his great surprise it was a young man so sick and emaciated that he resembled a corpse.

"Let me help you, my friend," said Francis. "Perhaps I can take you home."

"No, thank you, Bernardone," the other answered. "I need to walk a little every day to regain my strength."

Francis was startled that the stranger should know his name. Then he recognized him.

"Gallo!" he cried. "I haven't seen you for years. You've been ill."

"It's my lungs," he said. "I've been in bed for thirty months. Why don't you dismount? Let us sit by the road and visit. It is good to see you."

Francis and Gallo spent an hour together while the older boy told about his troubles. He said that his invalid mother had died nearly four years before. A neighbor and a visiting priest of the Order of the Cross Bearing Brothers had cared for him in his sickness.

"Thirty months is a long time to lie in bed and think, Bernardone."

"Yes, I'm sure it is," said Francis. "Tell me, are you still advocating revolution?"

30

"No," he answered carefully. "I am convinced now that what we need in our generation is a spiritual awakening within the church. Do you believe that, my friend?"

"Yes, I believe that," Francis answered slowly. He was thinking of an afternoon nearly six years before when he had trudged homeward along this same road, discouraged and confused, trying to solve a spiritual problem of his own. *It is still unsolved,* he thought sadly. Then for a short moment his countenance brightened as he recalled that first day he had seen his black filly.

"Gallo," he said, "I want you to feel free to ride my horse anytime you like. It will be good for you to take long trips into the country."

In the weeks that followed, Gallo accepted the invitation. Often he and Francis sat and talked together on the most serious of themes. Then, one day, Gallo startled his friend with a calm announcement: "Friend," he said simply, "I have only a little while to live. My strength is waning. I want you to know that *I have peace within my heart.*"

"I believe you mean that," answered Francis.

"I was never more serious in my life," Gallo continued. "Yesterday at confession the Savior was strangely near. He has become very real to my soul." He paused, apparently weighing his words with great caution. "I have learned many things in my meditation. I am convinced now that I can't purchase my salvation. Christ took care of that on the cross. It is free; yet there is much that one must do to prepare himself to receive it. Tell me, does that make sense to you?"

"I think so," answered Francis slowly. He was thinking hard upon that saying, longing for peace within his own breast.

A few mornings later, in a bleak little room that faced a filthy alley, Gallo was found dead, a pool of blood upon his pillow. A hemorrhage in the night had strangled him. Even so, there was that about his countenance which bespoke the infinite serenity of peace. It was nearly two weeks before Francis returned to his frolicking friends of Assisi.

31

In the months that followed, Francis became especially friendly with Bernard Quintavalle, his wealthy bachelor neighbor. Bernard was now in his thirties; Francis was approaching twenty.

"Bernard," Francis said to his friend one day, "why have you never married?"

"There is no good reason, I guess," the older one answered. "I've been busy all my life and away from home so much that I never got around to it. And now that I have prospered, the ones who obviously vie with one another for my attentions are not those from whom I would want to choose a partner for life. Why do you ask?"

"I'm not sure," said Francis thoughtfully. "I suppose that I am getting to that age. Sometimes I long to be wed to one to whom I could devote my life, all of it, forever."

"That's a noble thought coming from the son of Pietro," Bernard smiled. "Perhaps you will find just such a female who likewise will devote herself wholly to her husband."

So it was that Francis began to seek for the girl of his dreams. Many there were of that younger set (of which Francis was always the life of the party) who longed for his special smile, but none were of that perfection that his sensitive soul required.

Then came the war between two cities. Perugia was well situated with an army much larger and better equipped that that of her antagonist. But the noble sons of Assisi, blinded by their patariotic zeal, excitedly prepared for battle. Foot soldiers, dressed in gay colors, flanked by the prancing steeds of cavalry, paraded before the adoring women and children of the city. Francis, astride his black mare—she could no longer be called a filly—looked a little frail beside the others, but none was so smartly dressed nor well-equipped as this son of Pietro. Swords held high gleamed in the noonday sun, shouts were hurled, songs were sung, and a noble army marched out of the city to a tiny, bloody, medieval theater of war.

Alas! Hordes of horsemen, equipped with javelins, swords and shields, charged out from Perugia. Ghastly and altogether unexpected was the massacre of the first few minutes of battle as proud Assisi fell.

Francis, riding hard with sword raised high, was surrounded quickly by four Perugian horsemen. Aware that he was outclassed and outnumbered, he reined his steed to a halt to find himself looking into the manly face of an officer.

"Put down your sword, Son." There was a sympathetic note in the soldier's voice. "We don't want to hurt you."

Francis obeyed. "What are you going to do?" he asked.

"We are taking you prisoner."

"But what about my horse?" cried Francis. "She has been mine for years. May I take her with me?"

"There is no place for a horse in the prison." The officer was speaking as kindly as possible, for he saw that the young man was bravely fighting tears. "But I have a son who is thirteen; he is crippled. I will take your horse to him. He will ride her, give her a good home, and care for her as you would do. That I can promise, for you can see that our little war is nearly ended."

"Thank you, sir," said Francis, quietly dismounting. He handed the reins to the soldier. "I am ready to go now."

The Perugian prison was a dreary place filled already with Assisi's wounded, bleeding, blaspheming soldiers who, only an hour before, had ridden bravely into battle. Francis, unhurt and cheerful, went about the business of binding their wounds, befriending one who had incurred the disfavor of the others, smiling, sometimes laughing, and after the manner of Father Joseph, spreading an artificial sunshine where it was greatly needed. Prison without the smiling Francis would have been intolerable. Every dragging week would have seen quarrels and fights, sickness and infection, discouragement and death. Francis never faltered in his task.

After a long dreary year of incarceration, every man was alive and healthy when the dispute between the cities was finally settled and the prisoners released. Strange indeed was the sound of their singing as they followed the inimitable Francis through the gates of Assisi to be met by mothers, wives, and children whose faces were wet with tears of joy. Pica could hardly control her feelings as she ran to Francis' fond embrace. Mother and son walked home together, supremely happy.

Francis had celebrated his twentieth birthday in prison. The stormy teens were past.

3

To Kiss a Leper

It is not easy to understand how Francis could retain his health and good spirit throughout a year in prison, then, after returning to the luxury of his home, nearly lose his life with a lingering illness. But it was so. For months he lay upon his cot, burning with fever. Pica cared for him as tenderly as any mother could do, applying such remedies as she knew about and saying innumerable prayers in his behalf.

Through the long weeks of his convalescence he had little to do but meditate. Mostly he dwelt upon the long talks he had had with Gallo two years before, recalling again and again a statement his friend had made with fervor: *I want you to know that I have peace within my heart.* This was disturbing to Francis for within his own breast there was only turmoil. And another saying that he remembered was: *The Savior . . . has become very real to my soul.*

Francis was ready to exchange anything for this peace, but again he remembered how his friend had said, *I am convinced now that I can't purchase my salvation . . . It is free but . . . one must prepare himself to receive it.* There was something about these words now that touched a sympathetic chord in Francis' memory. For days he struggled with the problem, trying to recall some incident from the past that must somehow relate itself to Gallo's strange utterance. *Or was it strange?* he asked himself. *Hadn't Saint Paul expressed the same sentiment in his letters to the church?*

It was at this point in his meditation, one morning, that Pica entered the room and said, "A courier just brought news from your father. He will be home in a few days and, no doubt, will bring us lovely gifts."

"That's it!!" cried Francis. "I remember now!" Two great tears trembled upon his lower eyelids.

Pica stood in amazement, for never had her son expressed any particular emotion upon hearing of his father's return.

"Thank you," he whispered.

Pica, fully aware that she would never understand her strange son, withdrew quietly. Francis was aglow. *I see it all so plainly now,* he mused. *How did I miss it before?*

He was recalling the day that he had begged his father to let him purchase the graceful black filly. But Pietro had said, "No, she is already purchased and paid for. She is my gift to you as soon as you prepare to receive her."

Prepare yourself! Prepare yourself! was ringing in Francis' feverish brain as he tried to recount the sins that he must bare at the confessional. Over again he asked himself, *What must I do to really be ready for holy communion?* Gladly would he sell all that he had and give to the poor. Surely he believed on the Lord Jesus Christ. "What lack I yet?" he cried aloud and Pica came running to his side.

"Never mind," he told her. "I was sort of dreaming, I guess."

Again she left the room, her confusion mounting. Then Francis received the answer to his question. *Why must he so detest the lepers? Were they not God's suffering children?* Ah, this was a sticker.

"I will try, Lord," he whispered. "I will try, and someday I shall succeed."

Slowly the fever left, and Francis arose from his bed to make his way unsteadily to the patio. Two days later he went out-of-doors for the first time to meet a stranger who approached the steps. The man was tall and handsome with something familiar about his appearance. He studied Francis closely.

"Yes, you are the one I am looking for," the stranger said. "You are the young cavalryman we captured outside Perugia and took to prison."

"Yes," cried Francis. "My horse! You took her to your crippled boy!"

"That is right," the other answered. "My son grows weaker and can no longer ride. He asked me to give her back to you. It is probably the last favor I can do for him. She is down by the market. Now that I have found you I will have her brought to you at once."

Francis, weak from the fever and flooded with joy, took the man's hand in his own and wept like a boy.

Pope Innocent III was waging war upon his enemies in southern Italy. Walter de Brienne, Prince of Taranto, a gallant hero whom Francis admired greatly, was leading an army for the pontiff and needed all the reinforcements he could get. It was an Assisian knight who called for volunteers to help the warring de Brienne, and Francis, having regained his horse and some of his strength, answered the call to arms again. He was determined to become a hero. The shiny black mare appeared as spry and strong as ever; and Pietro, still proud of his son, equipped him again with the finest outfit available. Then Francis rode off with the soldiers.

Beside him rode a brave young knight, who through great valor, had won his spurs. But he was poor and shabbily dressed, and his altogether insignificant appearance beside the flashy Francis was more that the latter could bear.

"Do you see those trees ahead to the right of the trail?" Francis was pointing. "Let us pull up our steeds and hide there for a moment. I have something I must give you."

When they were hidden from their companions, Francis stated simply, "We must exchange clothing. It is not proper for you to ride into battle, a proud and noble knight, while I, whose only military record is a year in prison, appear to be a much better soldier."

The knight's first reaction was negative, of course, but Francis, already disrobing, would accept only yes for an answer. So the exchange was accomplished, and the two men caught up with their companions and rode until nightfall.

After eating around an open fire, the men rolled up in their blankets and soon were sleeping soundly. But Francis, wide-eyed in the darkness, was startled suddenly by a voice from the night. It was male, melodious, and firm. He described it later as the audible voice of God.

"Go back to your city," was the divine command. "I have work for you to do. Your orders will come."

Francis dared not disobey. So, dressed in the old clothes of the poor soldier, he mounted his horse in the darkness of early morning and made his way back to Assisi. Eyebrows were raised, questions asked, and rumors started; to all of these he paid no attention, as once again he assumed leadership of Assisi's younger set. But the old carefree days were gone. His conduct was above reproach and his conversation was that of a perfect gentleman. And there was a sadness about him because he could not say, "I have peace within my heart," with the same finality he had sensed in Gallo's witnessing words.

Then, one night when the battle within his breast was raging with special fury, Francis tried to withdraw from his friends. Sensing that he was under some kind of pressure, the others began to question him pointedly but received no satisfaction. So they turned to jesting, as the young are prone to do, and accused him of having fallen in love.

"That's it," he answered with enthusiasm. "I have fallen in love with the purist, richest, most beautiful girl in the world. One day I shall take her as my bride."

The others laughed. "He was jesting, of course," they said.

While Francis had spoken in figurative language, he had not been jesting. Lady Poverty was to be his bride. He had just then received a vision of poverty that was neither ugly nor painful—not the poorness that comes from losing one's savings at a gaming table, but a richness that is derived from giving everything for the sake of Christ. Someday he would claim his bride; but just now, peace of heart was an illusive commodity. It made him morbid, which was contrary to his nature and, therefore, a matter of real concern to his family and friends. The following day he wandered alone among the trees overlooking the vale of Umbria but was blind to all beauty. He felt the weight of the world upon his shoulders.

The awful depression that lasted for days then, apparently of its own accord, began to dissolve like the mists of dawn, and the sun shone through again. In his despair he sought no counsel, for he knew no one could help him. But now that it was over, at least for a season, he decided to visit his friend and confessor, Bishop Guido, whose mind was filled with the best of common sense. The bishop listened attentively, but unable to share the other's emotions or see his visions, he moved with caution, advising the young man to bide his time, to give heaven opportunity to make his pathway clear.

"What you need is a holiday," said the wise churchman. "Why don't you take a trip to Rome? It will do you good."

To travel alone was not safe in thirteenth century Italy. Bands of robbers, hiding along the roads, were ready to pounce upon any lonely wayfarer who dared to venture forth. But luck or Providence or both smiled down upon Francis as he polished his silver bridle rings. Bernard Quintavalle sauntered over to the Bernardone residence and found the young man grooming his mount in the little stall that Pietro never ceased to brag was built by his son at the tender age of twelve. Actually it had been repaired so many times that quite likely not one of the original boards or nails remained intact.

"Preparing for a journey, are you?" Bernard asked. "You wouldn't be wanting to go to Rome, would you? I have a small caravan headed that way the day after tomorrow. We will be happy to have you join us."

"Thank you! Oh, thank you!" Francis could hardly believe what he was hearing. "Of course I will go along. I was afraid I would have to wait for weeks to join a party. I have been making ready in case an opportunity came."

"What are your plans?" Bernard asked. "I have never known you to journey to any of the cities before."

"Bernard," Francis said with an earnestness that caused his friend to listen with rapt attention. "I am going on the advice of Bishop Guido. You see, I have had a feeling lately that heaven is preparing a special work for me to do."

This was probably the last thing that Bernard Quintavalle expected ever to hear. *The carefree Francis, son of Pietro, of all people,* he thought, *becoming a religious fanatic?* "Francis," he said aloud, "I am most anxious that you join our little party." He welcomed an opportunity to assist the young man back onto the road to reason.

The journey was a pleasant one as the little cavalcade walked its horses along the Tiber with Francis keeping the others entertained with stories. He was still very much at home on the center of the stage. Then one bright noonday he was told by Bernard to spur his horse to the top of the hill to look down for the first time upon the ancient city. He did, being glad to be alone for that great moment.

The Rome upon which Francis gazed was vastly different from that which the tourist sees today. The Colosseum and the forums were standing deep in the dust of the ages. There were art treasures to be sure, but Michelangelo, Raphael, and Di Vinci were not to be born for two hundred fifty years, and the dawn of the Renaissance had not yet begun to glow on the eastern horizon.

"Rome is quite a place," said Bernard as he reined up beside his young friend. "It is as ancient as the hills and as modern as the church will allow it to become."

There was a barb in his remark, the prick of which was felt keenly.

"Bernard," Francis said, trying to hide his irritation, "I know you think that I am crazy. I can't help that. But isn't it true that if it were not for the church—imperfect as she is—Rome would be buried and someday forgotten? Her legends would be accepted as myths and her history, pure fiction? I must give my thanks to God."

Bernard responded to this bit of oratory with a friendly laugh. "I doubt that it would be that bad, but every man to his own philosophy," he said. "I'm still going to thank the old she-wolf that suckled the famous twins." Bernard was trying to be funny rather than nasty or sacrilegious. It was all a part of his determination to save his friend from what he believed would be a dreary life, bringing great unhappiness to himself, his family, and his friends.

The little argument was interrupted at this point by a steady clicking noise, the unmistakable warning of uncleanness sounded by lepers. Approaching with hesitation was a man, old and decayed; his ears and nose were swollen into grotesque shapes: a gaping hole marked his naked shoulder as he held out a crippled hand for alms.

Bernard quickly dismounted, walked to the unfortunate man, and gave him a coin. "Poor fellow," he said, "I wish I could do more to help you."

Francis, his nostrils catching the nauseating stench of the sick one, became ill—he always did—and quickly urged his mount to some nearby shrubs. Jumping to the ground, he hid himself from his friends and vomited profusely.

Later, as the little party rode into the city, Francis pulled up beside Bernard and said, "My friend, I would give everything I will ever own if I could imitate you in just one thing."

"What do you mean?" asked the other.

"I mean," said Francis, "that I can't stand the sight and stench of a leper. Someday I will do what you just did, for God will help me."

Bernard was deeply impressed by this confession. Since pity was all that he had ever felt for the lepers it was difficult for him to appreciate Francis' problem, but he sensed his deep sincerity. And it was all a bit confusing, for he was beginning to wonder who was saving whom from what.

Francis and Bernard walked across the courtyard to Saint Peter's Basilica. Until recently, both had been strictly nominal in their relationship to the church. Bernard still was. Once inside, they made their way toward the altar where they knelt beside a half dozen others in silent prayer. Before them was a grating; beneath it lay the ancient tomb. Francis noticed that the others, including Bernard, dropped a few small coins through the grating which to his generous

41

soul, seemed to be miserly gifts indeed. Acting upon impulse, he opened his wallet and emptied it completely. The rattle of many coins attracted the attention of everyone. Bernard could hardly believe his eyes and later reprimanded his young friend severely.

"I will admit," he said, "that too many gifts are small, but why should you or anyone give *everything?* Tell me, how are you going to eat without money?"

Francis smiled with sheer joy. "You have heard, haven't you, that I am engaged to Lady Poverty? Isn't it well that she and I should get better acquainted before we marry?"

Without answering Bernard changed the subject, explaining that his business would keep him occupied for the remainder of the day. "I'll see you tonight at our camp," he said.

Francis' eyes were laughing. "I have business, too," he answered. Then they said their good-byes.

As soon as Bernard was out of sight, Francis hurried over to a beggar who was sitting dejectedly on the steps of the basilica. When anyone came near him, the poor fellow would hold out his hand hoping for a penny. As Francis approached he made the familiar gesture.

"I have no money," said Francis. "I wish to beg, too. If you will see that I get some old clothing, I will give you half of all that I receive today."

Soon the carefree son of Pietro became the most ragged and aggressive beggar on the steps. "In the name of Christ," he said to everyone. He was still thin and wan from his weeks with the fever, and few people had the heart to turn him down.

When evening came, Francis dressed himself in his traveling clothes again, and, having purchased his share of groceries, walked nonchalantly into camp. Bernard was confused, for he knew that his young companion wouldn't steal.

Finally the little caravan began its homeward journey. Bernard, who had hoped to effect a change in Francis' thinking, was aware that he had gotten nowhere; and he wasn't

42

sure that Francis was the one in whom a change was needed to be wrought. Then on the last day of the journey, he witnessed a scene that convinced him that a change of tremendous magnitude had come to Francis which had nothing in common with his own plans at all.

Francis had ridden on ahead of the little cavalcade presumably to be alone with his thoughts. When Bernard missed him, he became uneasy, for they were in rugged country, the most dangerous portion of the route. There was a switchback in the trail ahead which made it possible for Bernard, by turning sharply to the right, to ride down into a deep ravine and up onto the road again and intercept his friend. Turning to the others of the party he spoke sharply, "I don't have to tell you that this is dangerous territory. Keep together and follow the trail with caution. I'm going to cross the canyon to meet Francis. I'm afraid he is in for trouble."

Down into the rough hollow, between jagged rocks and stunted trees, his sorrel stallion made his way, nearly unseating his rider. Then up the other side, the faithful steed climbed steadily until they approached the road again. Bernard guided his mount to a spot behind a great boulder from which vantage point he could see the road without being detected. It was there that he decided to wait, watch, and listen without venturing out into the open to jeopardize his own safety unless trouble presented itself.

After a few moments Francis came riding around the bend into plain view. In that same moment a footman appeared on the road from the other direction. He was not a robber. The unmistakable clicking bespoke the fact that here was another leper; and Bernard, deeply interested in his friend's reaction, watched closely.

Francis, startled by the gruesome figure, was tempted severely to close his eyes, hold his nose, and spur his mount to pass the sick one as quickly as possible. But he didn't do it. "Lord," he whispered, "the time has come." Swallowing hard he dismounted, squared his narrow shoulders, and bravely approached the leper. He hesitated for an instant, then took the stubby hand in his own and raised it to his mouth and *kissed it*.

In an instant Francis could hardly contain his joy; great tears glistened in his eyes and every hint of nausea left him. He realized that he loved the leper—loved all lepers—and his love for God was boundless. It was then, in pure joy, that he embraced the sick one and placed in his hand the remaining pennies from his begging.

The leper moved on up the road sounding his warning of uncleanness to a world that was supposed to be well and happy. Bernard waited several minutes until Francis was out of sight. Then, urging his horse up onto the road, he overtook his young friend and rode along by his side.

Francis turned to him and said, "Bernard, I have built my stall and manger."

"I don't know what you mean," the other answered.

"Of course you don't. Someday I will explain it to you. But right now I want you to know that *I have peace within my heart.*"

"I believe you," answered Bernard softly. "I believe you."

4

Repair My House

Back in Assisi, Francis, loyal to his church, made his way to the confessional, then awaited further orders from heaven. His joy in the days that followed was unspeakable except in sober moments of meditation when he sometimes sensed his spiritual immaturity. On those occasions he longed for a love of God that would so transcend his love of self that the latter would fall into second place without hesitation or reservation. He was still engaged, but not yet wedded, to his Lady Poverty.

The church in every generation has had its seekers after perfection. Francis became one of them who was to find it. Honest, earnest Christians often seek a perfection that is unattainable in this life—an experience in which all love of self must be utterly destroyed, projecting body, soul and spirit into an ethereal realm, while continuing untouched on the road to heaven. Invariably, along this way, are two

45

enticing interchanges—one leading to marshy valleys of discouragement—the other, to mountainous regions of fanaticism. Francis might well have erred at one of these points if it had not been that selfishness had never been his problem. Hence, to him, this narcissistic tendency was not particularly condemning. So later in his search for the whole will of God, he never lost sight completely of the utter importance of self-love for Jesus had clearly inferred its necessity in His admonition to "love your neighbor as yourself." So, to love God *more than self* in every attitude of life became the "perfect love" for which he sought and which he finally attained. Even so it wasn't easy, for often in later years he was cruel to "Brother Body."

A great bank of clouds was developing in the west, and flashes of sheet lightning gave warning of an approaching storm. Francis, gazing out his window at the threatening skies, pondered seriously. Now that his way of life was radically altered, he no longer felt at home in his father's house; and Pica, thin and wan, hastening toward an early death, needed relief from every possible burden. He decided to pack his bag.

On his way out, stopping by his mother's door, he saw that she was sleeping peacefully. He left a note of explanation promising to return often and left quietly, walking briskly to beat the rain. He made his way beyond the walls of the city to a little sanctuary known as the Church of San Damiano, where an elderly priest named Peter, a man of deep humility, had gained the young man's confidence and profound respect.

As he drew near, Francis noted that the little building was in ill repair and that the pastor's house was small. The aging prelate sitting on a bench beneath a tree in the garden, watched the youth approach. He arose and walked slowly toward the gate to meet him just as a flash of lightning brightened all they could see of the universe, and a clap of thunder shook the ground beneath their feet.

"Now what brings my young friend to Saint Damiano, carrying a pack like a common beggar?" The kindly Peter was smiling at his own bit of humor.

"Don't laugh," Francis said with great seriousness, "for I must become a beggar for the sake of our blessed Savior. I have left my home, Father. Please, may I live with you until I formulate my plans?"

"Of course, Francis, of course." The amiable priest was beaming with delight. "I shall be honored to have you share my humble quarters and remain as long as you wish. Come quickly before the rain begins to fall. I will show you your room and find some covers for your bed."

Francis moved into the tiny cubicle provided by the elderly divine, placed his few personal belongings on a wooden box in the corner, and hung his extra clothing on a peg behind the door. He was tired—too tired—as he stretched his slender frame across the pallet and listened to the first large drops of rain that splattered the roof above him. Relaxed in body, soul, and spirit, he felt that he had never known such peace before. Another peel of thunder brought great torrents of rain, and Francis slept a dreamless sleep that lasted far into the stormy night. When he finally awoke, the rain had ceased, and a great full moon was trying hard to penetrate the thinning clouds. It was yet two hours before the dawn, but Francis arose and made his way along the muddy walk to the little church, alone. Inside the gloomy sanctuary, only the light of a tiny blaze, flickering at the altar, dispelled the blackness. Near it, prostrated before a crucifix, Francis prayed with fervor.

"Great God," he began. "Great God, full of glory, and Thou, my Lord Jesus Christ! I entreat you to enlighten me and dispel the darkness of my mind, to give me a pure faith, a firm hope, and an ardent charity. Let me have a perfect knowledge of Thee, O God, so that I may in all things be guided by Thy light and act in conformity to your will. Amen."

This extemporaneous prayer so blessed his soul that he repeated it two more times, memorizing it. Later, he used it again and again. Only his voice had broken the stillness of the sanctuary. Following the last *Amen,* an awful, penetrating silence seemed to envelope his soul.

How long he remained motionless and quiet before the crucifix he could not remember, but when he finally raised his head, the dawn was breaking. Through the window he saw the sunrise blazing through the scraggly clouds. He rubbed his eyes and was surprised to see that the morning light was penetrating the building, the blackness melting away. It was then that he was startled to attention by a deep melodious voice that seemed to come from the crucifix. A few moments earlier he would have thought that another had entered the tiny church. Now he could see that he was alone.

"Francis!" the voice said, "Go! *Repair My house* which thou seest is falling into ruin."

For a moment the young man was greatly alarmed, but he felt the salutary effect of the voice so keenly that he was filled with a joy that nearly overwhelmed him. It was the second time, he said later, that he had heard the audible voice of God. Nothing, it seemed, would quell his ecstasy. He could hardly wait to tell his friend the story. After running from the church he found the aging priest in the garden again in silent meditation. Slowly the white-haired pastor raised his eyes to see Francis approaching in haste.

Squinting, he focused on the young man's face and said, "I can see a certain transparency about your countenance, boy, that tells me that the great God of heaven has been listening to your prayers. Maybe you would share your blessing with a tired old man."

"Yes, Father! Listen, please—I have a message from heaven! I am to repair your church. It is crumbling away, you know." Francis paused only to catch his breath. "I will obtain bricks and mortar and go to work. Surely you won't mind."

Peter smiled. "Just mind your orders from heaven, and they will become plainer as you go," he stated simply.

Francis was aware that there was hidden wisdom in the old one's words, but he was too naive to ferret it out. It was not until much, much later that he discovered the far-reaching implications of the Lord's command: "Repair My house."

After breakfast, Francis lost no time in getting started

with his work. All day long he cleared away the crumbling ruins in preparation for the sections of foundation and walls that he would soon be building. And all day long he sang— praising God and thinking fondly of his Lady Poverty. *Someday we will wed,* he mused with pleasure.

Early the next morning he was at his work again. It was then that he needed bricks and mortar, and these, he thought with some confusion, his Lady Poverty could not provide; *he needed money.* He didn't worry long, however, for he had always considered himself a sort of junior partner in his father's business, and when in need of extra funds, he would simply sell some goods. The indulgent Pietro had never reprimanded him seriously for this, so Francis decided to follow the old custom. But it was different this time. In the first place he needed much more money than ever before; secondly, he was to spend it for that of which his father would not approve. Throwing caution to the winds, he made his way to his old home where no one responded to his call; Pietro was out of town, and Pica had gone early to the market.

Francis saddled his black mare—she was fourteen years old now and beginning to show it—and loading her with bolts of expensive cloth from his father's stock, rode southward to Foligno. There, with little difficulty, he found a buyer, who, like all merchants of that day, proceeded to press hard for a bargain. Finally, in order to obtain sufficient funds to repair the church, Francis was forced to sell his horse, which took every ounce of his dedication. It is quite likely that he would have refused the offer if it had not been that he was aware that soon he would have to give her up anyway, for Poverty doesn't ride horses. So, fighting tears, as often he had to do, he put his arm around the shiny neck, ran his fingers through the soft black mane for one last time, and bade his faithful friend good-bye.

It was ten miles back to Assisi. Francis, his money tucked away in a bag that hung from his shoulder, had no choice but to walk the dangerous trail as terrifying fears assailed him. At no time in his life did the enemy of his soul rack up as many points against him as on the occasion of this ten-mile trek. In his vivid imagination, highwaymen were hiding behind every bush and boulder, and every bend in the road was approached with awful apprehension.

Then upon him came the bitter spiritual depression that had harassed him many times before. Tired and sore of body, he welcomed the sight of a small, smooth boulder beside the road upon which he could sit and rest his aching limbs. Once seated he leaned forward, hid his face in his hands, and groaned aloud. He felt that he must be the least of all the servants of the Lord, that he could never measure up to the standard God had established for him, that he had failed completely.

He thought for a moment of suicide and sensing a pleasant response, became greatly concerned. Wisely, he forced himself to pray again: "Great God, full of glory, and Thou, my Lord Jesus Christ! I entreat you to enlighten me and dispel the darkness of my mind, to give me a pure faith, a firm hope, and an ardent charity. Let me have a perfect knowledge of Thee, O God, so that I may in all things be guided by Thy light and act in conformity to Your will." He became still more deeply disturbed to discover that praying didn't seem to help him. Then he heard the clicking warning of a leper's approach. He didn't know it, but here was medicine for his soul. He arose, ran to the sick one, embraced him dearly, and placed a number of coins in the palm of his badly deformed hand. The depression lifted.

It was evening when Francis finally approached the tiny parish house at San Damiano where Peter met him in the garden.

"Now where did you spend this beautiful day?" the priest asked with great seriousness. "I thought you were working at the church until I went over to give you a hand and found that you were gone. My young friend, I have worried about you today."

"I'm sorry," said Francis. "I should have told you my plans, but you were asleep when I left this morning. Anyway, I bring the best of good news for the future of San Damiano."

Taking the bag from his shoulder, Francis proudly displayed the money he had acquired to purchase bricks and mortar and explained in minute detail the method he had used to acquire it.

The elderly churchman listened carefully, his countenance reflecting more and more a grave disturbance within his soul. By the time Francis had finished his enthusiastic account of the day's activities, the priest could no longer hide his irritation.

"Young man," he nearly shouted, his face flushing crimson, "not one penny of these ill-gotten gains will go into my church! Your father will be angry beyond all measure and, I think, with cause indeed! One cannot steal to build even the kingdom of heaven! Do I make myself clear, Francis?"

"Yes, Father." Francis was blushing too, stunned by the reprimand. "I meant no harm. Sir, you have my word— I will not use the money." The young man turned quickly away to escape an embarrassing situation and made his way to the church were he tossed the sack of coins up out of sight on the sill of a window.

The pastor of San Damiano walked slowly toward his house in agony of spirit. He loved Francis as much as he could have loved a son and feared that he had hurt him deeply. He tried to pray: "Forgive me, I have wounded a sincere soul. Heaven alone can heal that wound and reestablish our fellowship."

Inside, the aging prelate sat down heavily, angry with himself. "I will never learn," he murmured beneath his breath. "I will never learn. I am much too old for that."

Francis too was scolding himself, aware too late that the priest was right. He realized now that Pietro would be angry indeed and suddenly feared his father's curse. *Money!* he mused angrily, *Dirty, filthy money! The very sight of it repels me! God hasten the day that I am through with it forever.* But his confusion was mounting; only money would purchase bricks and mortar, and he was under orders to repair His house.

Francis was engaged—but not wedded—to his Lady Poverty.

5

The Hiding Place

Francis went into the sanctuary where he spent the
next three hours in prayer. With great fervency of spirit
he besought God to teach him the way more perfectly,
to give him the mind of Christ in every decision, great and
small, to perform a reconciliation between himself and
the aging priest whom he had learned to love so dearly.
He finally decided to go to Peter to seek his full forgiveness, when he heard the door to the sanctuary swing on
its noisy hinges.

It was the priest, who, unable to sleep, had risen from
his bed to seek also blessed reconciliation. The elderly
divine carefully groped his way through the darkness of
the sanctuary to lower himself to his knees beside his
friend. There the two men prayed in silence until together
they arose to meet in fond embrace. Not one word was
spoken, for words are cheap when deep emotion trans-

mits thought for which there are no vocal symbols. Hot tears flowed from the eyes of age and youth alike, melting together two great hearts in a bond that could never again be broken. Either one would gladly have laid down his life for the other, and no greater love than that has any man. Nor did they end their silence even as they walked together to the house, for to risk the breaking of the spell which held them with such strange ecstatic power was unthinkable.

Later they ate their breakfast together, and no mention was made then or ever of the problems of the previous day or of the precious moments when those problems were resolved.

"Tell me," Francis broke the silence, speaking out of deep concentration. "What shall I do when my father comes?"

"Ah, lad, when you are fully prepared you must go out and meet him." The priest was speaking, too, from the depths of solemn meditation.

"But I am not prepared," said Francis, "and that, in itself, must be an awful sin."

"Nay, my boy," spoke the wise old Peter. "Neither was the great apostle ready to face his tasks at first, you know. He went alone to Arabia where he and our blessed Savior got together and solved the problem. You see, Christ had no trouble understanding, for He had found it necessary to go through Gethsemane before He faced the cross."

"Arabia is a long way from here," said Francis seriously. "Do you mean that I should go there?"

"Of course not, lad. It would be most impractical. Don't you see? Do you suppose that there is nowhere else that one might find a *rendezvous* with God?"

"What are you suggesting?" the young man queried.

"Well, now that you ask," Peter said with an air of mystery, "I do believe that heaven foresaw your predicament long, long ago, and in the great divine plan your answer was all worked out."

"This is hardly a joking matter," Francis spoke with a touch of irritation. "I must hide where I shall not be found until I can fast and pray to gain the spiritual strength that I will need from Christ Himself."

"Ah, have no fears," the priest assured him. "Old Peter never jokes when stern matters are under discussion. I have never been more serious than now. What I meant was that only a few hundred yards from where you sit there lies an ancient cave. It has no beauty and would be dangerous if children knew about it. Practically no one knows of its existence. Today I shall take you there and we shall place a pallet on the earthen floor. When the day arrives that you must seek seclusion, we will make provision for meat and drink to reach you daily, and you will be safe from every adversary except, of course, the devil himself. Now do you understand me?"

Francis bowed his head. Except for the adoring Pica, he had never known such friendship as that which he enjoyed at San Damiano.

Back at his old home, Pica was reclining in her favorite chair on the patio. Devastating, terminal disease had fastened itself upon her. The poor woman had neither any way of knowing what was wrong nor how to relieve the sharp jabs of pain that came more and more often. She longed for Francis. Then she heard footsteps on the gravel; but, alas, they were not her son's. Pietro was returning home unexpectedly.

When she heard her husband's voice she arose quickly to greet him but became so dizzy as to nearly fall headlong upon the floor as she groped for her chair. Pietro hurried to her side.

"My dear," he cried with real sympathy, "you are ill! What can I do to help you? Perhaps there is medicine in Paris!" It was plain that he was groping desperately.

"No, Pietro," she answered simply. "There is no medicine. Nothing can help me except that I would be so relieved if our son were here. Please go find him and bring him to my side again."

"Francis is gone," Pietro asked in amazement, "and you don't know where he is? Frolicking with his friends, I'll wager, and you about to faint from merely standing to your feet! Yes, I'll find him! And you may be sure that he will not leave you alone in my absence again!"

"No, my dear, you do not understand. Our son now serves our Lord and has gone to live with the old priest at San Damiano." Pica was measuring her words, trying hard to catch her husband's reaction. She knew that soon he would know the truth anyway and felt that it would be best for her to tell him.

Pietro flushed with anger. "So! He has become some sort of fool and has ridden off on his horse, leaving his mother alone in her illness! He must love that animal more than I suspected," he said hotly.

"No, my husband," Pica went on cautiously. "Francis sold his horse together with some goods from the store to purchase bricks and mortar to repair the church. He left me a note saying that I would be better off without the burden of preparing his meals and tending his clothing. He is doing what he believes is best for all. Please bring him to me, Pietro, and don't be angry with him. He wanted no money for himself—only for the church. He loves poverty more than riches and vows to be poor for the sake of heaven."

Pietro's anger was approaching the bursting point. Without a word he went to the stockroom where quickly his experienced eye told him that some of his most expensive wares were gone. Stomping back to the patio, screaming, cursing, forgetting Pica's problem completely, he swore to teach that smart young culprit a lesson to carry to his grave. "I'll beat him within an inch of his life! I'll make him wish he had died in battle to bring us honor, not disgrace!"

By this time Pietro was swinging his arms and yelling so loudly that all the neighbors heard him. Pica had seen him angry on other occasions, but never before had she seen the bulging purple vein on his forehead which now appeared about to burst. She became greatly alarmed and more so when she heard him cursing and threatening like a madman. Out-of-doors he made his way with great determined strides toward his steed to head for San Damiano, too upset to notice that another horseman had preceded him through the gates of the city.

The first rider was none other than Bernard Quintavalle,

spurring his stallion in a determined race to warn his young friend of his father's wrath.

Francis was busily excavating beneath a broken wall of the church when he heard the pounding hoofs of Bernard's stallion. A moment later Quintavalle reined his horse so sharply that the huge animal reared high upon his glossy hind legs and bared his great white teeth as the bridle bit tugged unmercifully at his tender mouth.

"Whoa, boy. Take it easy there." Bernard spoke soothingly as his mount settled back on all fours, trembling, foaming from the strenuous race. Far behind came Pietro, his tired horse in an easy lope.

"Bernard, my friend," smiled Francis, "what brings you in such a sweat to San Damiano? Surely you aren't about to ask me to accompany you to Rome again so soon."

"No, Francis, I have come to warn you! Pietro is on his way here. He seems to have lost all reason, and I fear for your life!" Bernard was speaking with great haste. "I don't pretend to understand all this, my young friend, but I can't stand by and see you flogged to death by an angry parent!"

"Thank you," spoke Francis calmly. "Ride back quickly and meet him. Tell him that I am no longer here. It will be true—I promise you—by the time you reach him."

Quintavalle turned his horse around and walked him slowly down the trail just as Pietro came into sight.

"Quintavalle!" Pietro was still fuming. "What were you doing at San Damiano? Is Francis there?"

"No, Bernadone," the other answered quietly. "I was told that he no longer resides with the priest, and I do not know where he has gone."

Pietro, apparently not satisfied with Bernard's feeble explanation, rode on to the little church. Peter, watching from his window, saw the angry parent approaching and hurried from the house to meet him.

"Where is that boy of mine?" Pietro demanded hotly, reining his mount to a halt.

"My friend," spoke Peter calmly, "Francis was here for a while but now has moved on again. He promised to return later but until then I doubt that you shall find him."

"I'll find him!" vowed the angry Bernardone. "And when I do he will pay for every transgression of his life! Maybe you didn't know that he got the money to fix your crumbling church by selling goods that he stole from my warehouse and that he sold the horse I gave him to buy bricks and plaster!" His voice had reached a high crackling pitch. "Sir, I warn you! If you are shielding that boy, I'll face you before the bishop, and you'll find out that the name of Pietro Bernardone is to be feared in Assisi!"

"Now, now," cooed the frightened divine, "Francis did not spend the money he obtained from selling your goods and his pretty mare. He knows now that he did wrong and still has the money somewhere. I shall do my best to get him to return it to you the very next time I see him. I am sure that, even now, he is thinking it over well. Please, my good man, exercise a bit of patience, and all will work out for the good of everyone. That's a promise from the sacred writings, don't you know? And one day you will be proud of the fine devout son that you sired, who already has reached heights of dedication to God that puts this servant to the shame."

"Bah," was Pietro's only retort as he swung his mount around and started up the trail toward town, sputtering to himself.

6

Strength for the Day

Peter went into the house to prepare a bowl of pottage, which together with a few simple utensils, he took to the cave. There, as he expected, he found Francis kneeling in the gloomy shelter, whispering to God.

"I knew I would find you talking with the Almighty," said the priest with a note of satisfaction. "Here, I have brought food and drink to sustain you."

"Only the drink, Father," spoke Francis with conviction. "I have a great battle before me over which I must gain perfect victory. I will fast and pray."

Fast and pray he did. For long days the pangs of hunger nearly drove him to distraction, but he refused to break his vow. Night seemed worse than day as he listened to a lonely cricket and the moaning wind outside the entrance of the cave. Some sort of crisis was inevitable, of course. One evening when Francis feared that he could not endure another hour, it burst upon him. He gave full vent to his emotions, crying out in agony of soul and body, taking refuge only in the thought that Christ, too, had suffered these temptations. Then sleep—blessed, blissful sleep—God's ancient anesthetic for his suffering children, was mercifully administered to the son of Pietro Bernardone.

The lowest ebb has always seen the turn of the tide. The morning light was seeping through the entrance of the cave when Francis opened his eyes to face another day. Everything seemed different to him. He said later that his soul overflowed with the splendor of a strange, powerful emotion—a magnificent sense of well-being. He believed that he loved God with a whole new passion, that he was ready to ask for the hand of his Lady Poverty, that now he really loved the whole world enough even to die for it. The gray walls of the cave, which through the dreary days had been so depressing, seemed to glow in the dim light with a hint of purple, amber, and gold. Even the cricket's monotonous song was melodious and lovely to the ear. *And the pangs of hunger were gone completely.* His mind had become as clear and sharp as high *C*, and truth—pure, unadulterated truth—was his to handle and to love. It set him altogether free.

Prayer, as he had known it, seemed less important now as he reveled in the very presence of the Almighty, and suddenly he came to understand with a whole new sphere of comprehension—the meaning of the petitions he had formulated and memorized one night in the nearby church. He repeated them aloud: "Great God, full of glory, and Thou, my Lord Jesus Christ! I entreat You to enlighten me and dispel the darkness of my mind, to give me a pure faith, a firm hope, and an ardent charity. Let me have a perfect knowledge of Thee, O God! So that I may in all things be guided by that light, and act in conformity to your will."

"I thank Thee, Lord," he said, "for granting these petitions in a most delightful fashion."

At home, Pietro, continuing to fume, made preparations

to take a short journey to Spoleta. Pica, following the foray with Francis, was worse and could hardly be left alone, so a woman was sought to attend her.

Word of Pica's illness and need of help passed quickly among her friends and reached soon the ears of a certain Ortolana whose late husband, Faverone, had been of the class of the feudal nobles. Ortolana had three daughters, Clare, Catherine, and Beatrice. They had been under the guardianship of a wicked, strong-willed uncle named Monaldo and lived with their mother in a magnificent fortress-like house near the piazza. Not withstanding all this, Ortolana was a devout and venturesome woman, having accompanied her husband on one of the Crusades to the Holy Land, and pursued as a hobby the growing of plants. She had the most beautiful garden in town. Her outdoor activities (she worked closely with her servants) tanned her skin and calloused her hands, robbing her of the beauty that could have been hers, if she, like many women, had made the most of nature's lavish provisions in her favor. Ortolana, who had profound respect and sympathy for Pica Bernardone, wished very much to go to her assistance. There were certain responsibilities at home that made it impossible for her to get away, but she took time to discuss the problem with her oldest daughter, Clare.

Twelve-year-old Clare was cast in the mold of her mother. Serious, devout, deeply religious, with clear honest eyes set in a remarkably pretty face, she listened with more than ordinary interest to the story of Pica's predicament.

"I will go, Mother," she said. "I would love to wait on such a lovely lady. Please allow me to go. It's the least that we can do."

"Yes, my dear," said Ortolana, "but be sure to come home as soon as that Pietro returns to town."

So it came about that Clare moved into the Bernardone residence and with tender compassion waited upon the ailing Pica. During one of the long periods when the two little women were sitting together on the patio, Clare asked many questions about Francis and his remarkable conversion. Pica loved to talk about her son, of course, but finally felt constrained to ask the reason for the young girl's apparent interest in him. And thereupon Clare, with nothing to hide, poured out of her childish heart a story that had never been told before.

"I've known Francis since I was six," she began, "when he used to let me ride behind him on his beautiful black horse. That was shortly after my father died and Monaldo took charge of Mother's affairs. Monaldo is mean—I've always had to fight to keep from actually hating him—and I used to cry for my father to come home. Mother always told me that he was alive in heaven, and I could never understand why he didn't come back and visit us. But he didn't come, so, to fill an empty place in my heart, I used to pretend that Francis was my older brother. I loved him exactly as a little sister should."

For a few moments Clare, with hands folded in her lap, sat quietly recalling scenes from her childhood. "I remember," she was reminiscing now, "how I cried when I saw him riding off to battle in the Perugian War. Monaldo saw me and whipped me for crying, saying that Perugia was going to win the war and he was glad of it. Then, when Francis was captured and put into prison, it seemed more than I could bear. I was nearly ten when he came home. Standing in the crowd, I wanted to run to him and call him Brother, but he looked right at me and didn't remember who I was. I had to fight again to keep from crying.

"I think that I was never so happy as when I heard about his great new faith in God. I'm sorry that his father is angry with him. Where do you think your son has gone?"

"I don't know," answered Pica honestly, "but I am sure that God will shield him, and someday he will come back to us."

In the days that followed, there arose a magnificent friendship between Clare and Pica. With it developed a strange mutual understanding until their silence became as vocal as their conversation. Neither could so much as imagine that any fault or shortcoming could possibly possess the other.

Their great love in no wise resembled a mother-daughter relationship—neither one had need for that—but it rather reflected the strange bond of affection that two soldiers, crouching in adjacent foxholes, suddenly feel for one another. It was beautiful to behold. Pica unconsciously drew upon it for much needed vitality, so that when Sunday came, she dressed herself and accompanied Clare to mass at the church of Saint Nicholas. They were supremely happy.

Back at the cave, Francis was preparing to conclude his fast. Loud and clear rang the voice of heaven to his now ultraperceptive mind. He was aware that his emaciated body had definite limits of endurance. He must put food into his stomach again. He dreaded the resulting cloudiness that would necessarily envelop his thought processes and shut out his razor-sharp communication with God. But he knew that he would never lose that which he had learned: the meaning of absolute poverty, complete dedication to God, and most of all, the needs of a lost and dying generation. He saw clearly his commission.

His former fear of Pietro seemed unreal and unimportant now. His course was laid; he had passed the point of no return; he was to follow God's plan for his life as long as life lasted. Then he would reap his reward in Paradise. This was the least of all his objectives.

When Peter came into the cave, Francis announced his decision. "Please," he said, "will you bring some goat's milk and tomorrow a bit of fruit and honey? The Lord has revealed many and great things to me, the last of which is that the time has come to end my fast."

Three days later Francis came out into the light of day and slowly propelled his weak, emaciated body up the rocky trail toward town.

"I must go alone to meet my father," he had told the priest. "I have no fear. God will not allow me to be tempted above that which I am able to bear. But please go into the sanctuary and pray, for just to know that you are there will help me."

Francis' heavy head of hair in contrast to his light, sparse beard was disheveled from his long sojourn in the cave. He tried in vain to comb it smooth, but it didn't matter. When he finally reached the city, his old friends didn't recognize him; and children, thinking that he was a madman, followed at his heels. *"Pazzo! Pazzo!"* they shouted, attracting more and more attention as shopkeepers and their customers came out of the stores to see the strange young man who had wandered into Assisi. The first to recognize him was Bernardo di Quintavalle.

"It is Francis di Bernardone," he stated simply, and the news traveled swiftly through the gathering crowd.

Insulting taunts, mud, and finally stones were hurled, but Francis did not care, for he knew that soon many of these adversaries would be repenting and turning to him to assist in their search for the smile of God.

Bernardo di Quintavalle was troubled with mixed emotions. He doubted the young man's wisdom but could not believe that Francis was crazy. Not being sure of anything, he held his peace.

Only moments earlier, Pica and Clare were visiting on the patio when Pietro appeared suddenly at the gate. He seemed deeply disturbed even though he was yet unaware of the strange drama in progress on the street a few blocks away. He growled in response to Pica's words of welcome, which reminded Clare of her mother's words of warning. She sought immediately for an opportunity to gracefully excuse herself and hurry to her home just as the sounds of the jeering crowd jolted the three to attention.

"Pazzo! Pazzo!" floated in on the afternoon breeze, and Pietro hurried out to share in the excitement.

One must admit that Pietro's humiliation upon seeing his son an object of scorn was understandable; but his angry, unbridled cursing as he pushed through the throng to snatch Francis by the wrist and slap his body to the ground was another matter. The crowd would have interfered except that a parent's rights were well established in Assisi.

Francis offered no resistance. *No retaliation* had become his motto and the great rule of his life.

"Return my money!" bawled the irate parent as he stood over the prostrate body of his son.

"I am sorry, my father." Francis spoke without a hint of fear.

Pietro, beside himself with rage, reached down, grabbed his son by the shirt front, and pulled him to his feet. Had the frail young man offered the least resistance, he would have been marched home like a naughty six-year-old child, for Pietro was a powerful man. The gaping crowd was plainly disappointed as Pietro and Francis walked along together, the latter aware that he was in for the threshing of his life. It didn't matter. Francis found joy in the thought that whatever stripes he might receive would not be unlike those administered to Paul and Silas and even unto the Lord himself.

When the loud jeering of the people gave way to silence, Pica walked to the gate with Clare to bid her good-bye and thank her for the loving assistance she had rendered. The two women were blissfully unaware of what had stimulated the fracas until they saw the father and son walking up the drive. Francis flashed a smile at his mother, then studied the face of the young lady at her side.

"I ought to know you," he said simply. "Yes, I remember now. You were the little girl who used to like to ride my horse. Your name is Clare."

"Yes, Francis," the girl replied without a hint of shyness. "I pretended that you were my big brother, and I have said prayers for you every day for years. You may be sure that I shall continue." Then she bade them all good-bye and hurried down the street toward her home.

Pica, weak and trembling, shocked by the appearance of

her son, knew well that a terrifying experience awaited as she followed Pietro and Francis into the house.

7

A Day in Court

Francis' punishment was accomplished with a heavy leather thong, and unmerciful indeed were the lashes that cut deeply into his back and shoulders as Pica screamed and tugged at her husband's arm. Finally, the young man fell to the floor, unable to rise.

Then the enraged man turned upon Pica—the best friend he had ever known—and with the back of his big brown hand, slapped her across the face so hard that she fell fainting to the floor. Leaving her there, he dragged Francis to a dark, damp room in the cellar beneath the great house where he placed manacles upon his wrists and locked them securely. Then he returned to Pica, splashed a dipper of water upon her ashen face to revive her and carried her to her bed.

It was then that a thin, shifty-eyed young relative of Pietro's named Angelo appeared at the gate. For years he had worked part-time at the dry goods counter and often stayed at the Bernardone residence. Angelo hated the slightly younger Francis and that day had thrown the first stone. He hated everyone, even Pica, who always cared for his needs and called him Son. He would have thoroughly enjoyed the tragic drama of the past few moments but, fortunately for all, had not arrived in time to see it.

Pietro saw the young man standing at the gate, picking nervously at a rash of red pimples on his neck and face, afraid to venture closer. "Angelo!" Pietro roared. "Go get that Clare girl again to stay with Pica. I'm leaving town. Would that I might never need return!"

Clare took over the care of Pica again, bathed her aching body, fixed broth with vegetables and meat which she carried daily from the market, and kept cold towels upon her feverish brow. The poor woman was delirious and much of the time thought that Clare was Francis—a little boy again—coming in to beg for food and to talk and laugh about his friends.

Poor Clare, carrying a load too heavy for one of twice her age, grew tired to the point of exhaustion. Often she would drop off to sleep while trying to care for some simple task, only to be awakened with a start by Pica crying out in her delirium. But finally there came a night when the ailing woman slept peacefully through the lonely hours allowing the faithful girl for once to enjoy unbroken rest. But in the early dawn the girl was startled to attention to find Pica wide awake, sitting upright in her bed.

"Francis! Francis!" the mother called. "My son, where are you?"

The girl hurried to the woman's side.

"Oh, Clare!" cried Pica. "Tell me, where is Francis? What did Pietro do with him?"

Clare, relieved to discover that Pica had regained her senses, could hardly contain her pent-up emotions. She wanted to cry or laugh or both—it didn't matter. She knew that if ever a cool head and steady hand were needed, this was the hour. She found control.

"Francis is in the cellar," she said. "He's coming along fine. I have bathed his stripes each day; he is eating well, gaining strength, and is anxious to be loosed."

"Oh!" cried Pica. "The manacles! Pietro must have put him in the chains!"

"Yes, Pica." Clare spoke steadily. "He is in the chains."

"The keys!" cried the mother. "The keys! In the cupboard by the stair! Get them quickly! We will go down and set him free!"

Clare found the keys, but Pica was much too weak to stand.

"It's all right," said the girl. "You stay in bed; I will release him."

And so she did. For one last time Francis and his mother were together, and such a reunion as they enjoyed can hardly be described. But greater troubles were lurking in the shadows. The chalky whiteness of Pica's face and hands bespoke a problem much too difficult for medieval medicine—or modern medicine, even—to resolve. Francis, always an optimist, was unaware of the devastating symptoms. The women plotted together to keep the gravity of his mother's condition a secret, and they kept it well.

"If you are strong enough, my son," said Pica from her bed one morning, "you must go to the work that God has given you to do. I will miss you, but you have my blessing and my prayers. I would not want you to delay, even for a moment."

So Francis returned to San Damiano.

Peter was delighted to see his young friend again. "Tell me," begged the priest, "about the ordeal that our great God has allowed you to endure. Were you able to accept it in good grace?"

Francis gave a complete account of the days and nights of suffering he had known. He told of the faithful Clare who brought ointment to ease his pain and broth to give him strength. "God has His hand upon that girl," Francis said with conviction. "There is a deep passion within her breast for those who suffer. And," he continued, "even at twelve years she has a radiant beauty that can be nothing other than a reflection of the love and passion of the Christ himself."

"There now," the priest began seriously, "I would like to meet this lass who has so completely captivated my young understudy. Perhaps it is good that she is yet a little girl."

Francis spoke sharply. "If this were anyone but you, I would greatly resent the inference. The only bride that I will ever know will be my Lady Poverty. We will wed soon. As for the lovely Clare, God has shown me that she shall live to bless the world as the Lord's handmaiden, pure and undefiled."

Francis, whose prediction was so prophetic as to dispel all likelihood of coincidence, was not to see the girl again for several years. He went back to his work of repairing the church, rising early, working late, singing, praying, and generally scattering sunshine to all who passed that way.

Pietro returned home to find Pica reclining on her bed of illness. Clare had gone to the market.

"Where is Francis?" he shouted, without so much as asking about his wife's health and happiness. "Is he still in the cellar, or have you set him free against my wishes?"

"We have set him free," answered Pica firmly. Her fears had left her for she knew that soon she would be released from all the cares of life. "He is back at San Damiano about his Master's business. You will do well to leave him with his work."

Pietro turned white with rage. "I'll show him," he screamed. "Son or not, no man can sell my goods and give the money to some fool charity! He will return my money, or this time I will turn him over to the magistrates!"

Out of the house he stomped, mounted his horse, and rode again down the rocky road to San Damiano. Francis was mixing mortar when his father rode up beside the church. With no further disposition to retreat, the young man boldly faced his parent with no semblance of either defiance or fear. Pietro, who had regained his

70

composure, decided to try a new tactic in a final effort to win back his son and save the honor of the name of Bernardone.

"Francis, my son," he said calmly enough, "please come home to your mother and me, and I will forgive the past and place you in charge of the store. And one day, of course, the business will be yours."

"No, my father," the young man spoke firmly. "I have no further interest in the business nor in ever going home again. My future is in the hands of God, whom I will serve with all my soul and strength as long as life shall last."

Pietro, realizing the futility of trying to reason with his son, lost all control of himself again. The distracted man sent forth a volley of oaths that hurt the boy much more deeply than the whipping had done, swearing to meet him before the judge. Spurring his horse unmercifully, he rode back to town. He did not stop until he reached the hall of the magistrates. There he preferred charges exactly as he had threatened to do, and soon a herald was on his way to San Damiano with a summons for Francis' arrest. But it was to no avail, for Francis had been advised by Peter to refuse the summons since he was now in the service of the church and therefore subject only to ecclesiastical authority. Later, when Pietro was told of this development, he made his way to Bishop Guido with all haste, demanding that Francis be brought before him.

Guido was a worldly priest, a man of means. He felt that Francis had gone a bit too far in his search for Lady Poverty, but he still had profound respect for the young man's courageous faith and dedication. It disturbed him to know that in the matter at hand he had no choice. Pietro was within his rights, so another herald was sent to San Damiano, and this time Francis accepted his summons without a word.

The day of the trial tingled with expectancy, for it was common knowledge that Pietro Bernardone would meet his son on the steps of the piazza before the mighty Guido.

71

Damp, chilly weather could not deter a great crowd from gathering, for the citizens of Assisi were seldom provided such exciting drama. It seemed, eventually, that everyone in town must have moved into the piazza.

Bernardo di Quintavalle was there. Numerous priests and monks appeared, many of them determined to make known that they would have no part of fanaticism. To prove it they were prepared to publicly ridicule the strange young man who lived with Peter at San Damiano. Ortolana and Clare were in the great crowd too, as were many of Assisi's younger set of whom Francis had so recently been the undisputed leader. Angelo was in the inner circle, picking at his pimples and making strange grimaces (he had developed a nervous twitching of the face) with plans to laugh and, if possible, to spit in the face of Francis of whom he was insanely jealous. Business rivals of Pietro were present also, hoping secretly that the elder Bernardone would suffer embarrassment and loss.

The vast majority of the throng, however, had no preconceived idea of who was right, nor did they care. They were there to watch a thrilling drama—the outcome of which no one could guess until just before the final curtain. Thieves and beggars moved in and out among the people as the huge crowd continued to expand beyond all expectation. It was a great day indeed in Assisi.

For two hours the people visited and laughed, passing bits of news, which before traveling far became grossly exaggerated. Then, as the crowd began to tire, arguments developed, and fights among the younger men seemed inevitable.

But all this ended with a murmur of approval when Bishop Guido, dressed in magnificent robes and turban, appeared with his servants to take his place in the judge's seat. Next came Pietro, a commanding figure, whose wealth and power were plainly evident in both his bearing and his dress. The crowd waited in silence for the appearance of a ragged, emaciated young man who, according to the rumors, had recently embraced some far-out fanaticism for which he would now pay dearly.

Then Francis appeared with the aging Peter at his side. The crowd gasped its surprise, for the young man had donned the brightest, most expensive clothing of his frolicking days, and his thick black hair was carefully groomed. He stood slender but straight, bold but humbled, serious but at ease.

Peter laid his arm across his young friend's shoulder, whispered a blessing and moved quietly into the crowd. Everyone, including Pietro was most favorably impressed—especially the bishop—as Francis moved forward with grace and beauty to face his father and the court.

What this return to his old self meant was a puzzle to all. A rumor spread quickly that he had given up his vows to God to return to his father's home and business. There were mixed emotions among the principals of this dramatic performance, with Pietro hoping and Guido fearing that the rumor was true. But the suspense ended abruptly as Francis addressed the bishop and explained that it would not be necessary for formal charges to be brought against him publicly.

"I am fully aware of my father's complaints," he stated calmly, "and I'm prepared to make restitution."

Turning to Pietro he tossed a wallet to the ground before him. "Sir," he said, "there is your money, every cent. Take it, I want never to touch the filthy stuff again."

Then to the amazement of everyone, he quickly disrobed, and, with only a rough loin cloth covering part of his slender body, he threw the clothing down beside the wallet with a dramatic gesture that spoke more loudly than his words. Pietro opened his mouth to speak, but Francis was not yet through.

"Sir," he continued, "until now I have called you my earthly father; but hereafter I shall say only, 'Our Father who art in Heaven, in whom I place my treasure, my confidence, my all.' "

His words rang with a note of finality; there was nothing more to be said. The crowd again murmured its approval, and the bishop, so deeply moved that he wept without shame, ran to Francis to embrace him, wrapping his own garment around the nearly naked body.

Pietro was a picture of despair. With shame and reluctance he picked up the wallet and the clothing, knowing that he had won the battle but lost the war. Angelo alone followed him out of the piazza as the multitude shouted angry taunts at the hapless merchant, who in an effort to escape quickly, stepped up his pace to a most undignified jog. His well-groomed head was pushed forward until his chin rested on his chest and his thinning iron-gray hair fell down across his eyes and face. At his heels, like a hungry mongrel, trotted the sickly, immature Angelo. Hardly could an artist portray utter defeat as clearly as was accomplished in this disgusting pantomime.

The audience turned its attention back to the center of the stage again, for one of Guido's servants, a laborer from the gardens, was replacing the bishop's robe, putting his own cloak upon the hero of the drama. Francis made a mark of the cross upon it and, motioning to his old friend, made his triumphant exit. This was the final curtain.

"This gardener's cloak is my wedding garment," he said seriously as Peter joined him. "I am wedded now to my Lady Poverty. 'What therefore God has joined together, let not man separate.' "

8

The Herdsman

Two mornings later, Francis and Peter, having risen from their beds at an early hour, were sitting together on a bench in the garden watching a glorious sunrise.

"I am about to take a journey," said Francis unexpectedly. "Far up the mountain in the town of Gubbio I have an old friend whom I wish to visit. I shall travel alone, depending upon heaven for every human need, for I shall carry with me only this scanty apparel which the elements and common decency dictate that one must wear."

The old priest, whose eyes were filling with a mist that distorted the beauty of the sunrise, tried hard to focus his gaze upon the young man's countenance. It, too, was aglow with the dawning of a new and beautiful day.

"My son," the old one said with great seriousness, "the depths of your dedication puts me and my worthless life to shame. Go—God will see you through. Never could I have mustered faith enough for myself to depend so fully upon the undeserved favor of heaven, but somehow I have no difficulty reaching through for you. You have my blessing and my prayers."

Hoofbeats in the distance warned the two staunch friends that visitors, even so early in the day, were approaching San Damiano. To their great surprise, they recognized the horsemen to be none other than Bishop Guido himself with one of his faithful servants.

The bishop dismounted and bade his friends good morning. "While praying in the early hours I felt constrained to ride out to visit one of my most loyal priests and my young friend, Bernardone. I was sure that I would find you at your meditation. *Come sta?*"

"We are well, very well," Peter answered fervently. He was greatly honored by the visit of his superior who stayed to breakfast at the little parish house at San Damiano. It was here that Guido was told of Francis' decision to take his lonely sojourn to Gubbio.

The bishop was less understanding than the priest had been, for he had lived too long in the lap of luxury and power to readily comprehend the sanity of such a seemingly senseless plan.

"My boy," he said, "take your trip if you will. But why must you travel without food or money? Will you not be tempting the Lord by placing such unnecessary hardship upon yourself?"

"No, Father," Francis answered without hesitation. "Any security that I might carry along would destroy my freedom. I would be burdened with fear again lest robbers would lie in wait to relieve me of my surplus. I fear, too, that God would be disappointed at my lack of faith. I must go just as you see me now; and since that means that I have no preparation to delay my departure, I shall bid you both good-bye."

Then, receiving their blessings, the young man rose to his feet and soon was on his way, singing, meditating, and praying as he climbed the upward trail. The trees were budding, the grass was green, and the birds, warbling their mating calls, seemed to welcome the happy stranger to their fields.

Onward and upward he went without pausing even to rest until late in the afternoon when he sighted a sheep rancher's cottage perched on the bank of a tiny stream. He quickened his pace, for both hunger and thirst pounced hard upon him, and two huge dogs, growling, snarling, and baring their fangs, dared him to come another step. But they didn't know Francis. Without a moment's hesitation he ran to meet the ferocious canines. His arms were extended as he talked and laughed and called them to come to him. The confused animals could smell no fear upon this strange innovator, and soon he was stroking their sides and rubbing their ears. He sat down upon the cool grass and smoothed the scraggly fur of their backs and rubbed their cold noses with the palms of his hands.

Then, rising to his feet, he boldly approached the house, accompanied by the two four-footed shepherds as they wagged their tails and licked his hands. A little boy, sitting on the doorstep, screamed at the sight of the unexpected visitor and ran into the house shouting the strange news. The rancher and his wife were busily sacking seed into small bags from which soon they would sow their tiny fields, when their excited offspring told them that a young man was approaching.

The grizzly herdsman, unable to believe that a stranger could get past his faithful dogs, hurried to the door with his good wife at his heels.

Francis greeted them in the name of Christ and quickly explained his mission. "I must have food," he told them simply. "I have no money, for as a child of God I am wed to Poverty. But I have trained and willing hands and I will gladly work."

"Come in." The man spoke a hearty welcome, surprising himself and his family, for never had he accepted an unknown traveler before. Francis had disarmed him with the same fearless frankness that had so quickly conquered the snarling dogs.

Together they ate mutton and vegetables, hard black bread, and tea brewed from sweet smelling herbs of the woods. Francis told them of the grace of God that had changed his life and filled his heart with joy. But neither the man nor his wife were ready to accept the witness of this strange young Christian. They were openly critical of the church and especially of a certain wordly priest whom they had known in other days.

"Ah, my friends," spoke Francis quickly, "to be at odds with the church is neither new nor surprising, for the church is the imperfect instrument of a perfect God. But if it becomes a more effective tool in His hands because we are a part of it, neither man nor God can say that we have lived in vain."

Then he told them of Gallo and his victorious life and death. "He convinced me," he said, "that I too must find peace within my soul." He told of his sickness, his trip to Rome, and his experience with the leper, as a tear slid down his cheek. He brushed it away with the back of his hand, but another followed and still another. He talked of the love of Christ and of the godly priest at San Damiano who took him in and nurtured him in the Christian life and of his extended fast in the cave. He became so absorbed in his own story that he seemed to forget his audience until the wide-eyed lad who had been hanging upon every word began to cry.

"Please help me, sir," the little one stammered. "I want to love God, too."

Then the boy's father laid a rough, hairy hand upon Francis' slender wrist and spoke with great seriousness. "Yes, my friend, our son is right. We all want to love God. What must we do?"

So Francis told the story of the stall and manger. "Prepare to accept His gift," he said simply. "Confess your sins, take the sacrament, and our perfect Christ will honor your faith." Then Francis prayed as great peace came to the heart of the herdsman and his house.

The good woman prepared a pad and cover upon which Francis slept through the peaceful night. Early in the darkness of predawn, he arose to pray and weep with joy. Through the day he worked at every menial task he could find as he answered scores of questions greatly expanding his witness. The following morning he bade his friends good-bye.

"I will see you when I return," he said with fervor.

"We shall be waiting for you," cried the host, "and may God bless."

9

A Trip to Gubbio

Higher and higher up the mountain, Francis made his way, singing and talking to the animals and birds as if they understood him. Perhaps they did. While begging his bread from the people of the hills he labored diligently and never failed to leave his witness. Only at the hut of a hermit was he denied entrance and aid; for the filthy, bearded recluse was a lunatic whose conversation was both vile and incoherent. So Francis went on, carrying mild pangs of hunger with him up the rocky trail. At higher levels the air became chilly, and tiny patches of snow still clung to the shady sides of knolls and trees.

The sun was lowering in the west when the lonely traveler came upon a lovely, level, partially wooded area in the center of which bubbled a spring of pure, clear water. Hundreds of small animal tracks in the surrounding mud bespoke the fact that this was a popular watering place. At the upper end of the natural trough the ground was dry and hard, and Francis found it easy to lie on his stomach and drink his fill after which he sat upon a fallen log to rest. It was strangely quiet, except for a sentinel bird in the top of the tallest tree, that emitted clear, shrill warnings to his wildlife friends. Francis sat quietly expecting that soon he would gain the confidence of the feathered sentry, after which little friends would poke their heads up out of their hiding places to make their own inspection. But it didn't come to pass. The shrill calls became more and more insistent as the agitated fowl left his perch to flit noisily from tree to tree. It was then that Francis realized that he was not the only innovator disturbing the peace of this lovely community. He stood erect to face the densest thicket, cupped his hands to his mouth, and shouted loudly: "Whoever you are, come on out of hiding. Your acquaintance we would make quickly and your friendship we crave."

His invitation was accepted in part. Seven rough men, one of whom was larger and perhaps a bit older than the others, stepped into the clearing. With hairy arms folded across their chests, they studied carefully the slight young man in the ridiculous garment of the bishop's gardener.

Francis threw back his head and laughed. "It's robbers, you are," he cried with glee. "Once I feared your kind, but that was when I carried valuables and was worth a handsome ransom. Now I own nothing, for I am wed to Poverty. I am a herald of the King!" He laughed again, opening his garment to expose his slender body, covered only with a scant undergarment.

"Fool herald!" the leader snarled. "Men! take his worthless coat and throw him into that bank of snow. And when he is frozen to the ground the world will be a better place!"

Before the men could reach him, Francis slipped off his outer garment and tossed it into their hands. Laughing, he ran and threw himself into the patch of snow. The men, confused and disgusted, turned back to the woods as Francis shouted that the Christ had forgiven a thief on the cross and would gladly do the same for them. Then he sought shelter among the trees, covered his shivering body with cool dry leaves and slept through the chilly night.

The next morning he awoke too cold to remain in his improvised nest. His arms and legs were numb; his head and back were aching. He struggled to his feet, brushed the leaves from his body, and began a slow jog up the rugged trail. But it was not until a warm Italian sun smiled down upon him that the coldness left his trembling frame.

Pangs of hunger were adding their torments as he reached an eminence from which he could see far in every direction. Francis spotted a many-windowed building nearly hidden in a large ravine and cried out with joy. Men in long tunics were working a garden, preparing ground for seed. They were followed by blackbirds searching carefully the moist black soil.

"A monastery!" he cried aloud. "Brothers who will gladly share their food and provide me with badly needed clothing!"

Then he ran down the grassy slope and hailed the startled monks in the name of Christ. Diappointment followed. In charge of the brothers was a tall stern friar named Julius who took an immediate dislike to Francis.

"Begone, beggar!" he said with an air of authority.

"It's true that I'm a beggar," said Francis solemnly, "a beggar for Christ. I have no money for I am wed to Lady Poverty, but I will work. I have trained and willing hands."

"You dare to talk of poverty," the friar sneered. "We are the ones who are wed to poverty by reason of our vows. But we don't go naked, begging food from those who owe us nothing."

"Nay," said Francis, "but your poverty is relieved by stores of food in your cellars. Is it not true that you know well whence your next meal comes? I have nothing but my faith in God. My dependence is upon Him day by day, aye, moment by moment. I stopped here because I believed that He would have you give me bread and clothing for which I will gladly labor at the most menial tasks."

Friar Julius fought to control his temper, for he felt condemned by Francis' words and forthright manner.

He sensed that his strange guest was making a favorable impression upon the humble brothers who stood by listening to this exchange of views on poverty.

"To the scullery!" he ordered. "Yours will be menial tasks, indeed! Food you may have, but clothing, no! Naked you came in your scratchy shirt! Naked you will go!"

So Francis labored over pots and pans as he sang and praised the Lord, all to the amazement and delight of the humble monks who secretly envied him his freedom. When his work was finished, he thanked the Lord, ate his fill of the coarse gruel that was provided for him, and after a night's rest, bade them all good-bye.

Clad only in the hair shirt he continued up the trail until he reached Gubbio. The first small dwellings that he passed were shacks, ill-kept and smelly, housing the city's poor, with naked children shivering in the doorways. They watched the stranger pass. They were amazed at his smile and gleeful song and, if they had been allowed to do it, would have followed at his heels. Farther along he passed the homes of Gubbio's more affluent, cultured society where backs were turned and doors were slammed, for to these people a maniac had apparently wandered in from the hills to invade their peace. Then an officer stepped out to arrest him.

Francis hailed the officer with a smile. "I am sorry, sir," he said, "to walk your streets—especially on such a chilly day—clad only as you see me. I was relieved of my outer garment along the way. Just now I seek an old friend who will minister to my needs. His name is Jacob di Arezzo."

"Arezzo," said the officer in surprise, "I know him well. Here, step inside this shop. You must hide yourself until I can find your friend and bring him to you. What is your name? That is the first thing that he will ask me."

"Tell him that once I was known as Francis di Bernardone, but I will be happier when I have forgotten that completely. Tell him, also, that now I am a herald of the great King."

Jacob di Arezzo came carrying a short tunic, a leather girdle, shoes, and a staff which Francis accepted gratefully along with an invitation to make his home at the Arezzo residence.

Jacob was a small man, shorter than Francis, with pale blue eyes and easy smile. His wife, Maria, was short, too, but decidedly overweight and remarkably jolly. Her wholesome laugh was heard often and far. The Arezzos were a happy couple except that their marriage had not been blessed with children.

Francis saw immediately that he was more than welcome and that his friends could well afford to keep him as long as he might wish to stay. But he didn't shirk his duty. Every morning, after a long, early season alone with God, he repaired the premises, prepared the garden for seed, carried fuel, and lifted every possible burden from the shoulders of his friends. Then, each afternoon, he made his way to the leper hospitals where he washed the bodies and cleansed the sores of the slowly dying victims of the dread disease. He began to feel that perhaps he had found his niche—that he should remain in Gubbio for life even—but two problems presented themselves soon which convinced him that such was not the divine plan.

The first problem involved his conscience. God had stated plainly that he should repair His house. Up to the time that he had left for Gubbio, Francis had been so naive as to believe that He meant nothing more than to lay new stone at San Damiano and, perhaps other churches in ill repair. He was still confused as to what the order involved. He decided that to find out he must return to San Damiano and complete the work that he had started. He had never forgotten Peter's sage advice: "Just mind your orders from heaven and they will become plainer as you go."

The second problem was a changing attitude on the part of Jacob and Maria di Arezzo. Francis sensed that they entertained fears that he might carry the leprosy. Since three so often constitutes a crowd, he knew that his welcome would not last forever.

So, one day, dressed in the tunic and belt that Jacob had provided (the shoes and staff he had given to a leper) Francis bade his friends good-bye and made his way back down the mountain toward Assisi and San Damiano.

By the time Francis approached the little sheep ranch again, the weather was warm; flowers were blooming, birds were singing, gardens were growing, and the pastures were deep and green. The two shepherd dogs, catching his friendly scent, bounded up the trail to meet him. Wagging their bushy tails and barking their pleasure, they jumped upon him to lick his face, landing four front paws simultaneously upon his chest and shoulders, sending him crashing to the ground. Down the grassy slope the three friends rolled, the dogs barking, Francis laughing, loving—life was good. At the house the welcome was equally enthusiastic. The herdsman and his wife prepared a sumptuous meal to celebrate the happy event, and the little boy clung to his friend with the tenacity of a leech. He told him that he had never known his parents to be so jolly and that the family prayed together every day.

"Yes, my friend," the father said firmly, "the Lord has heard our prayers. Not one ewe or lamb have we lost this spring, and our garden was never so rich and bountiful. You have been a wonderful blessing to us; your reward will be great in heaven."

Francis was anxious to get back to San Damiano; but since he was needed so badly, he stayed on at the ranch until the lambs were weaning and the hardest of the season's work was done.

Then he journeyed homeward to discover sadly that, in his absence, Pica had succumbed to the gnawing disease that possessed her.

10

I Should Preach?

At San Damiano Francis continued his work of rebuilding the walls of the ancient church. Again he needed stones and mortar but had no available funds. He smiled now at his earlier mistake of selling goods from his father's store.

"What shall I do?" he asked Peter.

"Ah, my son," the old one said without hesitation, "the Lord owns all the stone and mortar in the world. And his people, if approached properly, will fetch them and lay them at your feet. 'Ask, and it shall be given' was not idly spoken, you may be sure."

So Francis went into Assisi singing psalms of praise and promise. There were those who expressed distaste; but many of the townspeople, remembering the trial, were delighted. Children especially seemed to love Francis and followed at his heels. When a crowd gathered (as it always did) Francis, ever at home on the center of the stage, addressed the people regarding the needs of the church. His presentation was forthright without exaggeration; his appeals were irresistible.

"Give one stone," he would say, "and receive one reward; two stones, two rewards; and, of course, bring three stones and be thrice rewarded."

There was something magnificent about the unselfish response of the people. Beautiful building blocks, expensive and rare, were carried in and laid at the young crusader's feet. Passers-by paused to watch the happy mason at work, leveling, troweling, and all the time singing praises to heaven, as the run-down building became a thing of beauty. And always there were those who remained to assist with the arduous task, a labor of love.

"San Damiano," said Francis prophetically, "will one day be a monastery for women—females of the holy life—whose reputation will glorify our Father in heaven."

Late in the autumn of 1206, when Francis was twenty-four years old, the work at San Damiano came slowly to completion. However, an unexpected snowstorm which turned all that part of Italy into a sparkling winter wonderland, severely hindered progress in the final days. Francis was aware that this placed a hardship upon the aging Peter who prepared food each day for the loyal workers, and that the larder in the parish house was running low. So, back to Assisi he went, this time begging for food from house to house, offering always to repay with labor of any description.

Spring came early in 1207. Francis, having noted that another church was beginning to crumble away, was given permission to repair it, and discovered that his speeches requesting materials were increasingly successful. Seldom were the occasions when he was asked to pay for the stones and blocks that were brought in response to his appeals. One such request, however, was remembered by Francis as long as he lived. It was made by a selfish priest named Father Sylvester, whose gaunt frame and cold gray eyes bespoke the fact of his miserly tendencies. He came one morning, bending beneath the weight of a lovely slab of the finest marble. Francis was delighted when he saw it and said so with enthusiasm which encouraged the enterprising priest to ask an exorbitant price for the stone.

"You should know that I have no money," said Francis, "nor will I ever have money again. What I do, I do for the love of Christ and His cause. Were you not called to your holy office by this same Christ, and if so, do you not also owe Him everything? I do not ask that you give me your exquisite marble, but that you give it to Him, who loves you."

Two great tears glistened for a moment on Francis' lower eyelids, then slid slowly down his cheeks, melting the heart of the worldly priest.

"I'm sorry," Sylvester spoke out of deep feelings. "Perhaps you are right. I should give it for the love of God and His church. Take it and use it to His glory."

"Bless you," said Francis fervently, "you are close to the kingdom. I shall see you again." And see him again he did, for this was not the last, both bad and good, that he was to know of Father Sylvester.

While Francis pursued his vocation of repairing churches, his interest in the unfortunate people with the leprosy never waned. Every third day he would leave his industrious block laying to visit a leper hospital near Assisi. It was on these visits that he would stop to rest in a beautiful wooded area where stood the foundation of an old monastery in ruins and beside it, an ancient little church. The place was steeped in tradition. Angels, so the stories went, still came to worship there; but the last congregation of people to use the quaint sanctuary had deserted it more than a hundred years before. The monastery had been built nearly six centuries earlier than that by the Benedictine monks on a little portion of ground still known by that name, the *Portiuncula* (Little Portion).

Francis loved it. Here he found peace echoed in bird song and moaning wind. Hidden by vines, tinted with flowers, and scented by the perfume of the woods, it became to him a shrine more sacred than any spot this side of paradise. So he built a shelter near the tiny church where, through the lonely night, he prayed. His meditation, in tune with the lovely sounds of the warm Italian night, enhanced his love of

God until his soul grew in grace.

The little sanctuary known as Saint Mary's of the Angels became Francis' next project for repair. The building was constructed of huge stones which had stood the test of time. Above the ancient altar a fresco could still be seen on the moldering wall.

Francis, with great pains, slowly rebuilt this lovely shrine until people from the nearby fields gathered in to worship, when Peter came out from San Damiano to say the mass.

It was a Sunday in the winter of 1208 when Francis was twenty-seven years old that he entered the sanctuary long before daylight to sweep and dust and pray in preparation for the exercises of the day. The first footsteps he heard were those of the aging priest making his way along the bushy trail.

"I believe the Lord has given me a message just for you," said Peter abruptly. "After the mass I shall deliver my soul."

Francis was not surprised, for during the week he had sensed that the Lord was speaking to his heart. He was more than mildly aware that he had reached an important terminal in his walk with God.

The Scripture which Peter read that morning was from Matthew: "Do not acquire gold, or silver, or copper . . . or a bag for your journey, or even two tunics, or sandals, or a staff."

These words made a deep impression upon Francis, for already this was his dedication.

"Explain this passage, Father," Francis entreated the priest when opportunity afforded.

Peter enlarged briefly upon the sacred writings: "I think," he said, "that God has already made plain these truths to my young friend. But now allow Him to enlighten you further through the lips of a tired old man."

"Yes, go on," said Francis.

"Is it not true that the Lord spoke to you long ago saying, 'Repair My house'?" asked Peter.

"Yes, Father."

"And you did well to mind Him to the best of your knowledge," the priest continued. "I was certain at the time that He meant something much more important than the rebuilding of church walls, but I said nothing lest I should hinder the

Spirit in His leading.

"When you gathered the people around you to ask for stones, your appeals were most effective. My message, which I believe is right from God, is that you should gather the people around you again to plead for their salvation."

"You mean that I should preach?" asked Francis.

"Whatever you think," said Peter simply. Then he turned and walked away through the woods toward San Damiano.

11

Preaching Ministry

Francis returned to his shelter to fast and meditate throughout another of the most wonderful days of his life. He was competely enveloped—body, soul, and spirit—in the divine presence. He could say without blushing, "I was in the spirit on the Lord's day," understanding fully those immortal words of the beloved apostle. All earthly desires (he still had them, every one) were lost in his love of Christ. With perfect humility he became aware that he would be used of God to repair His house.

He was sitting with bowed head when a footstep in the leaves startled him to attention. Before him, not more than ten feet away, stood a girl in the full bloom of maidenhood, slender and straight, dressed in the purest white. He thought she was an angel. Her long brown tresses fell in soft, natural waves across her bosom; and her eyes, large and blue, gave life abundant to the most perfect features he had ever seen. Her expression was serious as she withheld a smile which Francis believed would reflect the pure joy of heaven.

"Francis," she whispered.

"Clare!" he cried, rising to his feet.

Alas! In the most hallowed moments of meditation the tempter is lurking in the shadows. In that instant an age-old impulse—one that had its beginnings in the Garden of Paradise—gripped man and maiden as he approached her, extending his slender arms. Whether the adoring Clare would have received his embrace was never known, for Francis, minding a sharp check of the Spirit, stopped short, dropping his arms to his sides. The girl smiled her relief as the burden of one of the great decisions of their lives was lifted from her adolescent shoulders. Francis had not so much as touched her fingertips; nor did he ever in the years that followed allow himself the pleasure of this one small indulgence. Neither did Francis nor Clare ever refer that emotion-packed moment again.

They sat and talked for a long time. Clare told of Pica's victorious passing as tears welled up in Francis' eyes. He owed much to his mother who had loved him—who through both precept and example had helped prepare him for the life he had chosen. Then Francis divulged his plans to repair the house of God, to revive the church. He explained too that he was wed to Lady Poverty as Clare gave close attention.

"God has revealed many things to me," he told her, "including the promise that San Damiano will one day become a convent where women with clean hands and pure hearts will serve the Lord with gladness. And long ago He showed me, Clare, that you are one of His chosen vessels. Please," he continued, "listen to His voice and follow in His steps. I perceive that in this hour He needs you—and me—even as we need Him."

"Francis," the girl spoke softly, "from the time I was a little child, I think I never wavered in my desire to do His will."

"Come to the *Portiuncula* anytime," he said, "where we will pray and plan together. But never come alone," he added wisely, "lest the rumors of men would destroy our effectiveness with God."

Nor had she come alone that day. Waiting at the little church in the woods were Ortolana and Catherine, Clare's mother and sister. Francis walked with Clare to meet them; then with deep appreciation he watched the mother and daughters, arms entwined, make their way along the trail toward town.

Francis soon was troubled in soul. He had been severely tempted when the lovely Clare appeared, pure and innocent, before him. This, to his ultraconscientious mind, was sin. At San Damiano he made his confession to Peter, weeping, referring to himself as chief of sinners. Then the wise old counselor set the young man's mind at ease.

"Our Savior was tempted, too, in every point as we are," he explained. "And you reflected His holiness when you, as He would have done, refused to yield to the tempter. It was with God's strength that you won the battle. You see, my son, it is not our temptations, but our sins, that must be confessed in godly sorrow."

This last statement by the humble priest became the theme of Francis' first sermon which he preached to a small gathering of townspeople near the marketplace in Assisi the following afternoon.

Unlike the screaming, radical, roadside evengelists who came and went in thirteenth-century Italy, Francis, dressed in a new garment of coarse sacking girded with rope, was every inch the gentleman that Pica had taught her son to be. His message, profound in its simplicity, was logical and clear, appealing to the intellect at the level of the people. Then, without trying, he appealed also to the emotions as his own deep feelings were transmitted to his hearers. This first message was just as effective, if not as polished, as most of the thousands of sermons that he was to preach in the years of his popularity.

He closed his message with an announcement that he would speak from the steps of Minerva the following afternoon. As the news spread, hundreds of people who had attended Francis' trial before Bishop Guido purposed in their hearts to be present to hear him.

Back at the tiny shelter near Saint Mary's of the Angels, Francis spent most of the night before God in praise and supplication. Toward dawn he slept the dreamless sleep of a tired child, waking only after the sun had flooded the world with light and the birds of the morning filled the woods with song. His mind was unusually alert and clear as long-forgotten Scriptures were called to his remembrance and God Himself became his commentator, revealing truths that neither priest nor scribe had understood so well before.

He put on his coarse garment with its attached hood, tied the rope girdle around his thin body, and made his way to San Damiano where he discussed his new vocation with his nearest, dearest friend.

"Advise me, Peter," said Francis seriously. "Today I need to tap your store of wisdom as I have never done before."

"My advice, son," the priest answered as he weighed carefully every word, "is no different than on that remarkable occasion when God first called you to repair His house: mind your orders from heaven and they will become plainer as you go. And that will never cease to be my counsel no matter how far you may progress or how important men may say you have become. Go now, fasting and praying, and God will speak through you to a multitude today. When it is over come back. I will have food prepared, and we shall sup together."

"Are you not going with me?" Francis asked.

"No, I must remain at home," the priest answered solemnly, "much as I dislike to disappoint you. I have hesitated to tell you this, but a pain attacks my chest and arm these days to warn me that the years are creeping up, and my old heart is growing tired."

Francis patted the old man's shoulder as he said good-bye. Then he made his way to the church to kneel before the crucifix where, one day, he had heard the voice of God saying, "Repair My house which thou seest is falling into ruin."

As Francis knelt he received the call anew. This time it was the voice of God within that spoke, but the message came with greater power than ever, and Francis entertained no further doubt as to its meaning. After an hour of meditation in which he gained much spiritual strength for the task at hand, he made his way up the trail to Assisi.

There, to his surprise, the square was filling with people—rich and poor together. He stood on the steps, spoke a blessing of peace upon the throng, and preached.

His clear melodious voice seemed to saturate the atmosphere as it rang with conviction. Pungent truth flowed through him to the people as faces of devout women glowed with rapture, and tears coursed down the cheeks of rugged men. Had he invited the hungry in soul to come forward after the manner adopted by many nineteenth-century evangelists, one can only guess what might have happened.

Then, two men moved out from the throng without invitation in search of that undeserved favor of God of which they had been told. One was a young lawyer, named Peter di Cantanei—the other, a wealthy, influential businessman known far and wide as Bernard di Quintavalle.

12

Bernard and Peter

Bernard and Peter had stood together throughout Francis' discourse. Both men were deeply affected, fearing that God was calling them to follow Francis in a life of poverty and privation to repair His decadent church. It was a great moment as Francis, seeing the two men move toward him, experienced an ecstatic touch from heaven.

Peter di Catanei cried out in the agony of condemnation. "I must find peace! Help me, Francis, or I shall die!"

"You are close to the kingdom," said Francis wisely. "Accept the pardon that was purchased for you on the cross. Repent—be willing to make it up to God—prepare for the gift of peace, and it shall be yours."

"I have been terribly wrong," said Peter honestly, "blaming everyone except myself for my problems, tearing down the very thing that needs repairing." He wept in godly sorrow; such was the moment of his conversion. Rejoicing, he went his way after asking his friends to meet him on the morrow.

Bernard di Quintavalle was troubled in soul. Hard indeed did he find it to accept the fact of Francis' utter abandonment of worldly possessions. He was tempted severely, asking himself whether this son of Pietro could be putting on an act to cover some ulterior motive. Such a motive, he reasoned, might be as pure and strong as the trill of the nightingale; but nothing in his estimation could justify the deceit involved. He had to know, for his own future hung strangely in the balance.

"Come home with me my friend, and spend the night where we can discuss this matter of complete dedication to God," he said so calmly that the other failed to guess the problem that disturbed him.

"Of course," answered Francis with appreciation, "but you must remember that I am neither seeking disciples not asking anyone to do what I must do."

"Good," said Bernard casually as he prepared to make the supreme test. "Perhaps I can make a liberal gift that would see your unique ministry off to an enthusiastic beginning and make it possible for you to give up begging to keep body and soul intact."

"Bernard! You shouldn't have said that!" Francis spoke sharply. He was hurt and showed it as he and his friend walked quietly toward the Quintavalle mansion. Once inside, however, the tension relaxed as again Bernard's questions were answered boldly until the two men retired for the night.

Bernard had ordered a bed for Francis moved into his own chamber. Then, to better study his strange companion, he pretended to soon be asleep.

Francis, longing to be alone with God in prayer, was most anxious lest he would disturb his host, so he too feigned peaceful slumber until he believed the other was settled for the night. Then, after slipping out of bed, he knelt in praise and supplication as an agonizing burden for Bernard's spiritual welfare settled upon his soul.

"My God, my God," he groaned in monotonous repetition throughout the dreary hours, not knowing that his friend listened with both reverence and amazement. It was nearly dawn when Bernard finally drifted off to sleep, awaking again when the sun poured through his window just as Francis concluded his lonely vigil and returned to bed to rest. By that time the last semblance of doubt of his friend's veracity had fled forever.

Later the two men had breakfast together. After retiring to Bernard's elaborate den, the wealthy nobleman turned to Francis and proceeded to state his case. He began as if he were about to make a business proposition involving a fortune—he was doing exactly that—as he might have done at a bargaining table.

"My young friend," he said, "the Lord has convinced me that your dedication to heaven's bidding has brought you a life of peace and service that Pietro's money could never have done."

"Those are your words," said Francis.

"I am further convinced," continued Bernard, "that unless I follow your example without reservation, only misery and loneliness await me in this life, and God alone knows what may be in store in the next."

"Those are your words also," came the simple answer.

"I have been made to shudder when I think of the wasted, unhappy life that must have befallen another rich young man"—Bernard was weighing his thoughts before allowing them to become words—"who one day turned away when the Lord commanded, 'If you wish to be complete, go and sell your possessions and give to the poor.' "

"I perceive," said Francis boldly, "that up to this point you resemble that young man very much."

"Yes, up to this point." Bernard was moving cautiously. "Francis," he continued, "I have never made hasty decisions. For many days now I have been pondering one of such magnitude as to make all others seem like a child's game of marbles. It is over now; my mind is made up."

"May God direct you," said Francis slowly. "Remember always, though, that no word of suggestion came from me. The devil, regardless of your decision, would pounce upon both of us in days to come if that were so."

"Now your words have become mine," said Bernard. "If you had brought the least measure of pressure to bear upon me, I would have reacted badly. My decision is being dictated by Christ himself. I will go sell all that I have, give the proceeds to the poor, and without reservation I shall follow Him."

For a few moments the two men sat quietly in meditation.

Bernard spoke again: "Since you have already done the same, Francis, I shall go with you. I will be greatly honored to be called your first disciple. As such I am ready for any advice you may wish to give me."

"It has been a long time," said Francis thoughtfully, "since I have made any major decision without consulting my old friend Peter at San Damiano. Let us go to him."

The aged Peter listened well to Bernard's story of faith and decision.

"Tell me, Father," said Bernard, "do you think that I am crazy? Could it be that the devil has persuaded me to take so great a step? I have come to you at Francis' suggestion, for never in my busy life have I needed the counsel of experience as I do today."

"Aye, my friend, and never have I been so happy to give a bit of advice as this opportunity affords," said Peter fervently. "The years have taught me many things. If you had offered to use your substance simply to support a reform movement—there are many such movements afoot today—I would be convinced that Satan was about his nasty business. You see, when a reformer appears on the horizon, he is usually surrounded quickly by a host of poverty-stricken people who are needy in every area of their lives. And the leader feels that his little crusade has heaven's stamp of approval because our Lord admonishes men to preach the gospel to the poor. But we must remember that our Lord's disciples came from among both the affluent and the oppressed, learned and unlearned, great and small. All, however, were poverty-stricken in a spiritual sense; and all, with one exception, became rich indeed in the sight of heaven. I have noted with interest that when today's revolutionary has amassed his band of hungry followers, then, a rich man is attracted to him, much ado is made about it, and the man's wealth is quickly appropriated to underwrite the movement.

"This in itself," the priest went on, "may not be bad except for another fact that must not be overlooked. The rich man unless he is a most unusual fellow, soon becomes a power behind the scene projecting his influence and making major decisions until the original leader becomes something of a stooge. Most of us are a bit stupid and slow to catch on. My hair was pure white before I realized that the church—whether the little parish of a humble priest or the powerful see of a mighty bishop—is upon its spiritual deathbed whenever it allows its wealthy men to do this.

"Bernard, my friend," said the priest as he leaned forward to study the man's reaction. "I became convinced long ago that God had placed His omnipotent hand upon our young friend Francis to repair His church. Now that his first disciple is a rich man, ready to become poor for the sake of the gospel, I am certain that my first impression was amazingly accurate. My advice to you, Bernard di Quintavalle, is without reservation. Go through with your plan, and God will bless."

Later that day Francis and Bernard met Peter of Catanei in Assisi, and the three friends went into the church of Saint Nicholas to meditate, pray, and search the Scriptures. The following passages—strangely related—seemed to project themselves:

"If you wish to be complete, go and sell your possessions and give to the poor, and you shall have treasure in heaven; and come, follow me." (Matthew 19:21)

"And he instructed them that they should take nothing for their journey, except a mere staff; no bread, no bag, no money in their belt." (Mark 6:8)

"If anyone wishes to come after Me, let him deny himself, and take up his cross and follow me." (Matthew 16:24)

Peter was deeply impressed. "My friends," he said, "I will be Francis' second disciple if he will have me. This way of life will bring me joy and permit me to be of significant service to God. Please, Francis, will you complete the rule by which we shall live?"

"Aren't the Scriptures plain?" asked Francis.

Bernard smiled. "Francis," he said, "your dedication to God is so complete that you cannot imagine that others may be less devout. Peter is right. Definite guidelines need to be established, and the rule enforced."

"I see," answered Francis slowly. "You are thinking that there may be some rich men who later will want to return to their former lives of ease."

"No," Bernard spoke firmly. "Our problem will not be with the wealthy. You and I have known the luxuries of life and, having counted the cost, are willing to bear it. The men we must watch will be those who have known nothing but poverty and have little to sacrifice."

Francis smiled his gratitude. "Not only has God given me a great commission," he said, "but with it exceptional wisdom through the knowledge and experience of my first two colleagues."

So eventually the Primitive Rule was established, the basis of which was poverty, chastity, and obedience.

The news that Bernard di Quintavalle was disposing of his fortune to follow God spread quickly across Assisi with many and varied reactions. No one was passive. At first Bishop Guido could not believe the report; then, convinced that it was true, he became deeply disturbed. He was a man of considerable means and an excellent administrator with a natural abhorrence for the impractical.

"Why, why?" he fairly yelled to Father Sylvester. "Why does a man like Bernard think he must become a common pauper to be religious? And why," he was shouting then, "if he must give away his money, does he not give it to the church?"

Sylvester had no answer, but there is little doubt that he shared the bishop's sentiments.

The Quintavalle fortune was soon reduced to cash, and a formal announcement was made that on the following day on the steps of Minerva all who were poor and needy would receive alms for the asking.

Bernard and Francis, each with large bags filled with money, stood on the steps of the ancient temple watching the stream of Assisi's poor—some diseased, ragged, and filthy; others clean, honest, but hungry and cold—coming with hands extended, whining, pleading, and pushing lest they should fail to get a share of the Quintavalle wealth. No questions were asked. Anyone willing to associate himself with this motley crowd was rewarded by the two smiling men whose glowing countenances, in contrast to the desperate faces of the poor, fairly shouted that it is more blessed to give than to receive.

Then up to the steps came a tall, gaunt figure in clerical garb trying desperately to avoid contact with the despised beggars who surrounded him. It was Father Sylvester who, one day, had tried to sell Francis a valuable piece of marble, then in an emotional response to the young man's quiet rebuke had made it a gift.

"Look," said Francis to his companion. "I'm afraid Sylvester's regeneration was not complete. I can tell by his step, Bernard, that he hasn't come to congratulate you on your generosity."

And so it was; the priest came whining. Since this money was being squandered upon those who had never earned a penny of it, he felt that he should be repaid for the exquisite slab of marble he had given to repair the wall of a crumbling church.

Francis listened with undisguised amusement. "Here, Father," he smiled, "take this double handful of filthy lucre. Tuck it away in your garment, for another handful awaits you. If this is not enough, we will give you yet another. If you must be cheated out of your blessing, we would not want you to be cheated out of the money too."

Sylvester accepted the gift, scowled, and hurriedly turned to leave, nearly upsetting a crippled man who with two homemade canes was struggling unsteadily up the steps.

"I feel sorry for a fellow like that," said Bernard. "He is a good man but terribly weak."

"What do you mean?" asked Francis.

"If he were not a good man," Bernard answered, "he would have refused to give the marble in the first place. And if he were not a weakling, would he have asked to be repaid? We should pray that heaven will grant him strength."

Bernard's generosity—stripping himself to abject poverty— had tremendous effect upon the poor people of Assisi, but greater than this was the response it invoked in the hearts of the more substantial citizenry. No longer did the people attend Francis' outdoor preaching services to satisfy their curiosity, but they came in ever growing numbers to hear his message of warning and promise. The church took on a new and vibrant spirit, for the church centers always in the hearts of the people; and the rising moral tone of the community became a fact ignored by none.

Bishop Guido's irritation at Bernard's disposition of wealth subsided as soon as he saw the healthy trend of the new movement. He gave it his personal endorsement; he was an honest man, big enough to confess that he had been wrong.

The third volunteer for discipleship was a plain, devout, and unpretentious man named Giles whose honesty and frankness soon became an icebreaker for the evangelists wherever they went. The brothers accepted Giles without hesitation.

Francis led his three companions down the wooded trail from town to the Little Portion where they improvised a shelter large enough to accomodate them.

13

Two by Two

From the vast number of persons revived in Francis'
informal services, there were always those who felt the call
to follow the brothers in their dedicated lives and ministry.
The first twelve Franciscans, all of Assisi, were named
Bernard di Quintavalle, Peter, Giles, John of Capella,
Morico, John of San Castanzo, Bernard of Vigilantia,
Sabantion, Phillip, Angelo, Barbaro, and Sylvester.

This last one named was none other than Father Sylvester
who came weeping to Francis and Bernard, begging
forgiveness for his wretched behavior in demanding pay
for his slab of stone.

"I have not had one hour of rest since that awful morning
on the steps of Minerva," he told them. "The money you gave
me I distributed to the children in the street. I have confessed
my sin to Bishop Guido and to God. Now I confess as humbly
as I can to you dear brothers. Can you find it in your

hearts," he cried, "to forgive me?"

It should be noted here that Sylvester never faltered; he served God and men with diligence and humility throughout the remainder of his life. He was the first priest among the brothers. This lay-clergy ratio of twelve to one, Francis heartily approved. Sylvester became the chapter's theologian and a great man of prayer whose counsel was valued highly.

The day came soon when Francis thought it wise to call the brothers together to discuss the matter of prudentials in discipline and dress. The plain sackcloth costume worn by Francis, complete with headgear and a girdle of rope, was adopted immediately as their official habit. It was neat but symbolized unquestionably the poverty to which they were bound. The only objection came from John of Capella who wore a hat and seldom was seen without it.

"There is nothing sinful about my hat." he argued hotly.

"No," said Bernard, "but since no poor man is ever seen wearing one like it, it becomes a symbol of affluency which is out of keeping with our ministry."

John, unconvinced, remained sullen putting a damper momentarily on the meeting. It was Giles who broke the silence.

"What about shoes?" he asked. "Only the wealthy can afford them. Sandals are worn by the upper middle classes; but the great majority of the people go barefooted. It makes no difference to me for I have never worn either shoes or sandals."

Francis came to the rescue. "Before our conversion," he said, "Bernard and I were never seen without expensive boots, and lately we have suffered from tender feet. But now, wedded to Poverty, it would be most unfortunate if we were to dress in any manner that the poor people cannot afford. And we have already become accustomed to the stones and thorns."

So it was agreed that both hats and shoes were inconsistent with the dedicated lives of the humble evangelists.

(For a time John of Capella bowed to the rule, but his discipleship did not last; it was easier for a wealthy man to give up many hats than for a poor man to give up one. On the day of John's departure, Peter of Catanei observed sadly that it would always be like that for the problem centered not in the hat, but in the heart.)

Francis closed the meeting with a little speech. "We have never sought disciples," he said, "but our numbers will grow. From England, Germany, France, and Spain they will converge upon us. It is for us to set a perfect example. When we are hungry we shall beg for food, but never without offering to pay for it with the work of willing hands. Since Italy's poorer citizens must barter, seldom so much as seeing a single coin, we shall labor accepting only the necessities of life; money we must spurn. The rule of chastity shall be most rigidly observed, abstaining even from the appearance of evil. Obedience shall be sacred, and we will countenance no less in any brother. Go then, the kingdom of God is at hand."

Such were some of the guidelines that were accepted gladly by those who came under the rule and habit of the order which later adopted the name of *Fratres Minores* (Lesser Brothers).

Stripped as they were of every worldly possession, the Lesser Brothers prayed and wept and laughed together at the Little Portion. But this could not last for long, for to pray and weep and laugh was not their mission, only part of their preparation for it. So Francis called the men together again to outline a plan of procedure.

"The gospel," he said with conviction, "has long been confined to the community of the church. We must take it to the people even as Christ sent His disciples, two by two, to the roads and markets and homes where lost humanity is always in abundance. So we shall go, north, south, east, and west with neither scrip nor bread nor money. We shall go singing, for everyone is seeking peace and joy. The merchant expects to find happiness in his profits; the robber hopes that stolen goods will lay it at his feet. We shall prove that we have found it in obedience to Christ. Brother Giles shall go with me. Peter, you shall accompany Brother Bernard. The rest may pair off as you wish, and a month from now we will meet again here at the Little Portion."

So they went their various ways, carrying the news of

salvation to a tired, cranky world that didn't want to listen.

"Brother Giles," said Francis as they prepared to leave the Little Portion, "let us go out of our way and visit a little sheep ranch where some good friends are waiting my return." Then he told of his experience on the road to Gubbio as Giles listened with more than casual interest, for he understood and loved rural people; they were his kind. Up a long slope the brothers trudged until they could see the little house on the bank of the glittering stream. Hurrying down the trail they were met by barking shepherd dogs and the young son of the rancher. No welcoming committee more genuine than this one ever existed, and the warmth of fellowship in the tiny house that evening made an undying impression upon these two evangelists.

"Our son," said the rancher proudly, "wishes to join you as soon as he is old enough to be accepted. He is a good boy and will serve with love and grace."

Francis flashed his fondest smile upon the lad. "God will bless you and make you a great blessing to the world," he prophesied warmly. "We shall be counting the time until you come."

"But what," asked the man, "is there for parents such as we? Hardly could my lady and I join the Lesser Brothers." He smiled broadly at his little joke.

"The Lord has shown me," said Francis, "that He will place His seal upon our labors with thousands of converts. For many days and nights now our prayers have been in behalf of those who obviously cannot join us. We believe we have received the answer, although many details must yet be worked out. It is quite likely that eventually there will be three rules. One for the Lesser Brothers, a second for Lesser Sisters, and a third for devout laymen like yourselves who will serve God with great humility in their various fields of labor. We shall develop our plans only as heaven reveals the way. To get ahead of the Lord can be more disastrous even than falling behind."

Giles, relating the incident later to some of the brothers, closed the account with the following statement: "I saw the weather-beaten ranchman reach over and lay a calloused hand upon that of his good companion as their faces glowed with rapture; the Spirit of Christ himself seemed to saturate the atmosphere of their humble home."

Generally speaking, the four weeks' mission seemed in no wise to be the successful ministry the brothers had anticipated. Heretics and fanatics with long faces, crying for revolution, had traveled these same roads, and it took time for the people to sense that here were crusaders of a different stripe. But they did sense it for no word of criticism could be wrenched from even the weakest brother. In answer to accusations against the church and clergy the happy warriors smiled and said, "Some of God's servants have not yet found the depths of His peace." But satisfactory response to their earnest witness was not forthcoming.

When the brothers met again at the Little Portion Francis detected at once that an air of disappointment had captured the spirits and dampened the ardor of the roving evangels.

"Tell us, Brother Peter," he said, "how you and Bernard were used of God on your journey of love."

"We failed," said Peter bluntly. "We failed miserably."

"Did you go singing and praying?" Francis asked.

"Exactly," answered Peter.

"When you asked for bread did you offer the labor of your hands with gladness?"

"Without exception, you may be sure."

"Did you greet the people with a blessing of peace and offer the news of salvation?"

"We did just that," said Peter, "but not once did we sense the joyful response we expected, nor were we asked to preach to the curious crowds that gathered."

Francis turned to face the others. "Tell me," he said, "does Brother Peter's experience describe your own?"

It did.

"Did any of you preach?"

Not one.

Then Francis smiled broadly. "We were preaching every step of the way," he said. "How blessed the man who does not walk the way counseled by the wicked nor linger on the paths of sinners . . . He is like a tree planted near running water that brings its fruit in due season." (Early Catholic translation)

How prophetic can a psalm become? Even as Francis was speaking, there approached a young man whose heart was full of woe.

"I must have help," he said, addressing himself directly to Bernard. "Not a moment of peace have I had since you came to the door of my shop with sunshine in your smile and hope in the promise of salvation."

Then, day by day, others appeared. With amazing swiftness the Lesser Brothers grew in numbers and in grace, for the gospel was being carried effectively beyond the community of the church. The message was unaltered—immutable God, as was, is, and shall be forever—but the brothers' method of propagating the gospel was as new as tomorrow and as old as Peter, James, and John.

14

Official Recognition

Not far from the Little Portion was a place called Rivo-Torto where Francis and his friends, in the poorest of improvised shelter, crowded together for prayer and rest. Among the many new disciples were Angelo of Rieta, Leo, and a never-to-be-forgotten little fellow named Juniper whose unrehearsed humor kept the brothers in stitches. (It was he whom Clare would refer to later as God's toy.)

But alas, the citizens of Assisi became disturbed by the growing number of happy beggars who had a way of appearing unexpectedly at their doors to ask for food and to talk without blushing of the salvation of the Lord. Numerous complaints began to reach the ears of Bishop Guido. The churchman was embarrassed, of course, but altogether unwilling to quell the strange movement, for the spiritual and moral tone of the church and community was rising to unprecedented heights. The church which had been falling into ruin was undergoing repair.

Then came an announcement by Francis that was as unbelievable as everything else about him. He and his inner circle of friends were going to Rome to seek an audience with the pope. They needed official recognition, he said, if they were to expand their witness. Bishop Guido was amazed at their audacity and suggested as a realistic alternative that they annex themselves to an already established order within the church. But whom would they join? There was only one *Fratres Minores*.

Francis feared the pope no more than he had feared the robbers on the road to Gubbio for, since he was wed to Poverty, he had nothing to lose. But Bishop Guido did fear the pope (he had much to lose). Therefore he hurried to Rome to prepare some of the cardinals for the strange visitors that were about to converge upon the Vatican.

Back at Rivo-Torto, Francis sent for Bernard. "We are going to Rome," he explained. "I have been there only once—the time you invited me to join your cavalcade—so you will be our leader. Please make arrangements at once."

Bernard laughed. "What arrangements?" he asked. "No horses, no money, no bags."

Francis' eyes were twinkling. "Do you remember asking me in Rome how I would eat after giving away my money at Saint Peter's?" he asked. "You never found out, did you, Brother Bernard?"

"No," the other answered thoughtfully. "I often wondered where you got the bread and meat that you brought back to our encampment."

"It was simple enough," smiled Francis. "I borrowed some old clothes and begged on the steps of the basilica. It was then I knew that I could accept the lepers as my brothers and kiss the hand of the next one I would meet."

"Yes, I saw you do it," answered Bernard. "To me, that was your greatest sermon; I was never the same again."

So, two mornings later with Bernard in charge, the brothers began their long sojourn to Rome, walking, singing, preaching, begging, working, winning souls. Guido was waiting to greet them.

Pope Innocent III was beset with problems of such magnitude as to make him feel that he bore the weight of the world upon his back. It should be said in his favor that he was a man of faith but with little time to exercise it. He paced the floor. On a particular afternoon he was pacing a huge hallway of the Lateran Palace groaning beneath his burden with face turned upward to the frescoed ceiling. Hence, he did not see the heavy door swing in a few inches to allow the entrance of a little man in a strange brown tunic of sackcloth, whose bare feet made no noise on the marble floor. Then, as lonely men often do, he began to sense that he was not alone. He dropped his gaze until his eyes fell upon Francis who stood with arms folded across his slender chest, resembling an elf that might have slipped in from the forest. The pontiff was so startled that he appeared ridiculous and, being aware of it, had to fight to control his temper. Certainly he was in no mood to grant any favors and quickly shooed the little man out of his presence with the tails of his flowing robes. But nerves are peculiar in their reactions, and the sudden fright left its impresion upon the mighty churchman, for in his dreams that night he saw the little man again. It appeared to him that the foundation of the Lateran Palace was crumbling; the walls were about to fall. He tried in vain to cry out, as men in nightmares always do, when the little man with the oval face placed his narrow shoulder beneath a beam and saved the building from falling.

Later when Pope Innocent related the details of the dream there were those who believed he had received a vision from heaven. Others said that he should break his habit of lunching just before bedtime; but all must agree that, whatever the explanation, that dream was to alter the course of history.

In the meantime, Bishop Guido had introduced the Lesser Brothers to the Cardinal of San Sabina, John of Saint Paul. The cardinal was a busy man who constantly waged a battle in high places to keep Christ in His proper place at the head of the church. Bishops, he contended, must be men who love God supremely; priests shall be living examples of Christianity at work. When a pope is chosen, he told his colleagues, it must be with the battlements of glory, not the battlefields of earth, in mind. John of Saint Paul was a great man, highly intellectual, deeply spiritual, and extroverted enough to take his stand on any issue where Christian principles were involved.

On first sight, the only thing about Francis that impressed the cardinal was the fact that Bishop Guido believed in him. He must have something, he told himself, so he entered into conversation with this strange young leader of men and, in so doing, was captivated completely by his humility, dedication, and apparent unlimited ambition. Later he asked the Lesser Brothers to remember him always in their prayers and begged to be granted an honorary membership in their order, whatever it might become.

Seeking an audience with the pope, the cardinal told him the story of the *Fratres Minores,* recommending them without reservation as dedicated servants of God of as nearly perfect humility as he had ever seen. "They preach salvation in its purest simplicity," he said, "altogether unlike the fanatics who are disturbing the people, doing violence to truth.

"Give them audience," he pleaded. "Bishop Guido has nothing but good to report of their evangelistic preaching and way of life."

Pope Innocent was impressed. Revival in the church of Rome was needed badly, and no one knew it better than the pontiff himself.

"Bring them to me," he said. "I shall see them."

So Francis and his friends, as neatly groomed as possible in their drab tunics, bowed at the feet of the mightiest of all the churchmen of the Middle Ages. They explained in the simplest terms their dedication to poverty and begged for recognition.

The pope was impatient. Unlike the cardinal, he didn't take the time necessary to be captivated by the humble evangelists and, having seen overzealous men before who took a way so straight and narrow that they failed later in their objective, refused the request.

"You are being too hard on yourselves, my sons," he stated simply.

"But Father," spoke Francis in desperation, "we are in the hands of the Savior, following His precepts and example. Must we fear that He will not provide us with the necessities of life?"

The pope remained firm. Speaking directly to Francis he said, "What you say is true, but your own dedication may far exceed that of those who follow you. You are asking men to take a way that is much too stern. Wait upon the Lord until His call becomes clearer and more realistic."

The interview was over. There was nothing more for Francis to do or say, so he and his friends left, deeply disappointed. But John of Saint Paul, who had stood quietly on the sidelines, remained to wage the battle for them. It was well that this cardinal was a favorite of Innocent's, for dangerous indeed were the critical words he directed to the pontiff.

"These men," he spoke with firmness, "have neither added to nor substracted one iota from the rule that Christ laid down for His disciples. If the way these humble evangelists are taking is too stern to be realistic, then we are saying that Christ himself is the author of fanaticism, and we are guilty of blasphemy!"

If the pontiff could have called to mind one argument with which to defend his case, it would probably have gone hard with both the cardinal and the Lesser Brothers. For a long moment he sat with bowed head and said nothing; there was nothing to say. Then, with a shudder, he recalled the dream of the falling palace and saw Francis again as the savior of the sordid situation.

"Bring them back!" he said.

So it was that the Lesser Brothers became *Fratres Minores,* having received official recognition from the pope himself who approved the Primitive Rule. "Go," he said, "and preach repentance. The Lord will guide you. Come back, my brothers, when your numbers have multiplied, and further favors will be granted you and greater missions shall be entrusted to your care."

15

Clare

The trip back to Assisi was without incident as the happy evangelists sang and praised the Lord, bearing witness to the saving knowledge of Jesus Christ to all who passed their way. When they reached the switchback in the trail, where Francis had kissed the leper's hand, they paused to bless the Lord.

"Go," said Francis to his companions for at least the hundredth time, "preach repentance. The kingdom of God is at hand."

Important news always finds a way to travel fast. Without benefit of wireless, rail, or airlines, the fact of Francis' visit with Innocent III and the subsequent approval of the *Fratres Minores* reached Assisi and was spread abroad long before the brothers came singing through the gates of the city. The welcome they received was without precedent. Prior to this the pulpits of the churches had been closed to the

Lesser Brothers. But now the invitation to preach, even in the cathedral, was extended to Francis, as one of the greatest revivals of history began. Asking forgiveness, paying old debts, caring for the poor, and putting an end to debauchery, wife-beating, immorality, and indolence became the new order of life across the length and breadth of Italy and beyond.

The Little Portion with its tiny chapel, Saint Mary's of the Angels, was turned over to the *Fratres Minores*—a gift from the Benedictine monks—to become the official headquarters of the order. The Franciscans were growing in every way.

Somewhere in every congregation that sat at the feet of the great evangelist could be seen his fondest admirer, Clare. The call of God to full-time Christian service (a daughter of Poverty) was strong upon her, a fact which she dared not share with her aristocratic family, except for her sister Catherine. The two girls kept the secret well as Clare tried to work out a plan to visit Francis at the Little Portion for the purpose of prayer and counsel. She had not forgotten Francis' warning not to come alone, nor would a girl have dared to venture unescorted beyond the protective walls of the city.

There was an older woman, a friend of Ortolana's by the name of Bona, who took a special liking to Clare and proceeded to help her. Bona was large and strong, capable of caring for herself in most any situation, so she and Clare were allowed outside the gates without question. Bona was not particularly religious but had profound respect for anyone who was.

"You really love the Lord, don't you, Clare?" she asked one day as the two friends were walking in the garden.

"Yes, Bona." Clare was speaking barely above a whisper. "More than all the world I love Him. When I see how He is using the Lesser Brothers I want to be a Lesser Sister; I believe it is His will. Mother would go along with such a plan if she dared, but Monaldo and the other men of our clan would tear their hair out if they so much as guessed that I plan to give my life to God. Monaldo has a fine young man of royal blood picked out for me to marry. 'A splended match,' he says, 'and providential.' He doesn't know what *providential* means. It's no use, Bona. I want only to be the bride of Christ, and Francis will always be my older brother. But I must have help, for I shall have to run away. I become sad when I think of Mother, but she knows that I shall be leaving home soon in any event and wants me to be happy. Catherine will probably want to follow me, for God has been speaking to her heart for many months, but she will have to wait to see how my plans work.

"Bona," Clare was looking straight into the older woman's eyes, "will you help me?"

"Of course I will," said Bona, surprised that Clare had felt the need of asking. "First, though, I think that we should talk with Bishop Guido, for unless he gives some indication of some willingness to recognize an order of Lesser Sisters or Poor Clares or whatever you and your girls will call yourselves, you will be defeated before you start."

"And just what are we waiting for?" asked Clare.

"We aren't waiting," said Bona, guiding their steps toward the garden gate. "We're already on our way."

Gaining entrance to Guido's study was not a simple task, but when finally maneuvered, the bishop listened with more than casual interest to everything Clare had to say.

"My daughter," he said with great seriousness, "Francis has already told me about such a possibility developing. God is working in a way most extraordinary with the Lesser Brothers, so hardly would I oppose an order of sisters if such should appear to be His will."

"Thank you, Father," whispered Clare.

"Go ahead and make your plans, keeping me informed," the bishop told her. "I will gladly keep your counsel, and when the time is ripe I'll see you through. May God bless you and your good friend also who is laying herself open to criticism and abuse to assist you in your purpose. Good-bye and good luck."

The following morning Clare and Bona, reporting only that they would be spending most of the day in the woods, made their way down the trail to the Little Portion.

The pine smell, unusually strong in the woods that day, was the breath of God to Clare. She wept with joy.

Francis listened gladly to her story, nodding his approval. "But we must not move too swiftly," he warned. "God is never in as big a hurry as we are. If we wait upon His leadership, all will work together for His glory."

For nearly a year the two women made regular visits to the tiny chapel where, with Francis, prayers were said and plans were laid until finally the date was set for Clare's escape from home to enter the service of the Lord. Clare, Francis, and the bishop were agreed that Palm Sunday would be a most appropriate day for the initial thrust of so significant an adjunct to the new evangelism.

Palm Sunday turned out to be a warm spring day, birds singing, bells ringing, children laughing. *The world is at its best,* mused Clare as evening settled down upon Assisi. Except for attending mass with her mother and Catherine, Clare had kept to herself throughout the long day lest her excitement should cause suspicion.

Clare and Bona waited until long after the family had retired for the night; then tiptoeing through a rarely used exit at the back of the house, they made their way quietly along the dark street and over the city wall to follow the well-known trail to the Little Portion. As soon as they entered the woods, the voices of the brothers chanting the matins at Saint Mary's of the Angels, fell softly on their ears. Francis' clear, strong tenor was easily distinguishable above the others.

"It is midnight," whispered Clare. "A new day is born."

"Yes," said Bona. "A whole new day for you. Just another Monday for me." There was an unmistakable note of sadness in her voice. Clare pressed her hand.

"You are the best friend a girl ever had," spoke Clare softly. "Serve the Lord with gladness and please say prayers for me each day."

"I will," said Bona. "Somehow you make me want to be really religious. I will be trying hard to please the Lord; pray that He will give me the peace that has long been yours."

As the two women entered the chapel the voices were hushed; there was solemn rejoicing. Two of the brothers led Clare to the altar where her hair was shorn and a long brown habit of sackcloth girded with a rope was wrapped about her slender body. The attached headpiece made an oval frame for her lovely face which was wet with tears of gratitude and joy. Then, when the service ended, Clare was taken according to Francis' order to a Benedictine convent a few miles away, where she would be cared for until further plans were laid.

Bona returned home exhausted. The first gray streaks of dawn appeared in the eastern sky as she crawled gratefully beneath the covers and slept the dreamless sleep of those who know that whatever men may say, God is pleased with their labors. But less than two hours later, her rest was rudely interrupted by Monaldo and three other men of Clare's family pounding on her door. Slowly she awakened as the incessant hammering continued.

"All right, all right!" she cried. "Quit pounding the door before you smash the panels! I'm coming!" She stepped into her slippers, pulled a silk gown around her large frame, and unbolted the latch.

"Where is Clare?" Monaldo demanded hotly. "You tell me where she is or . . . ."

"Or *what?*" she snapped. "If you had the sense of a braying jack, maybe she would still be home! Now get away from my door, or I'll break a chair over your marble head, and I'm in no mood for joking!" She reached for a chair.

Monaldo looked like a spanked kitten. "All right," he said, "you don't have to tell us. We'll find her if we have to twist the arms of every preaching beggar at the Portiuncula."

Bona realized that what he said was true; he would find out soon enough.

"I'll tell you where she is," she said boldly. "She's at Saint Paul's, on the road to Perugia. But you might as well give her up for she will never go back to her home again."

The men mounted their horses and rode off to the convent.

Clare saw them coming but didn't try to hide. As the men approached the Gothic entrance she swung open the heavy door and faced them squarely. They began pleading with her; then, losing their tempers, threatened to take her home by main force.

"It's too late," the girl spoke without a trace of fear. "I have left my home forever to serve God with all my mind and soul and strength." She raised the hood of her brown garment and exposed her shorn head, then turned her back and walked slowly down the long hallway, away from her angry kinsmen.

The men gave up. Clare and God, of course, were more than a match for them all.

16

Catherine

Catherine, a gangling, wiry damsel, physically and mentally tough, resembled her older sister only in her unwavering allegiance to God. When Monaldo came back from Saint Paul's after his futile attempt to capture Clare, the rest of the family cowered before his angry raving and idle threats. But Catherine paid no attention to him as she went quietly about the business of planning her own escape. She stood alone. Bona even declined to assist her, explaining sensibly enough that the family uproar over Clare made it expedient for her to bide her time.

"When you are eighteen I will help you," Bona promised.

"Yes, when I am eighteen," echoed Catherine with a note of bitterness. She went to her room, knelt by her bed, and prayed, pressing a small wooden crucifix to her breast. Her petitions were terse and deeply sincere as she turned her face dry-eyed toward heaven.

"Help me," she plead simply. "I cannot stay here longer even if I must run away alone."

Two mornings later, Francis, on his way to visit Bishop Guido, met Catherine at the steps of Minerva. He smiled broadly and paused, hoping to hear firsthand how her family was reacting to Clare's escape to a life of Christian service.

"Terrible," said Catherine in answer to his query. "And as soon as Monaldo takes his beady eyes off me I shall follow her. Tell me, Francis, will my sister remain at Saint Paul's? Is that where I shall find her?"

"No," he answered. "In a few days she shall be moved to the convent of San Angelo where she shall remain until final plans are made. I'm on my way to discuss all this with Bishop Guido now." Francis studied the girl closely. He was impressed by a certain fearlessness about her eyes and slightly protruding jaw.

"Whatever bit of common sense I have," he stated firmly, "dictates that I must warn you of the dangers you are about to encounter. But I can see by your face that I should reserve my counsel for someone who will listen." His eyes, if not his lips, were smiling.

"Thank you," answered the girl sincerely. "I shall appreciate the prayers of all the Lesser Brothers. God will see me through."

It was twelve days later that Catherine arose at four o'clock in the morning to slip quietly out of the house and over the moldy wall where Bona and Clare had made their escape. Along a little-used out-of-the-way trail to San Angelo, she ran through the night beneath ten thousand twinkling, friendly stars. She did not slacken her pace until the sun peeped over the eastern horizon. More exhausted than she realized, Catherine staggered to a level plot beside the narrow road where she lay panting as the cold wet grass brought chills to her perspiring body. Then she heard galloping hoofs and knew that a horseman approached from the direction she had been running.

She thought of Monaldo, fearing that he had discovered her plot and in a moment would demand that she return with him to Assisi. Too tired to fight, Catherine closed her eyes and prayed until the rider pulled up his mount beside her.

"Please, miss, may I help you? Why are you here alone?"

The voice sounded very young and kind. "Surely you must know that it is dangerous out here. Tell me your name; mine is Jacques."

Catherine opened her eyes to meet the wide-eyed gaze of a small boy not more than ten years old. She smiled her relief.

"My name is Catherine," she said. "I am on my way to San Angelo. But where would a boy like you be riding so early in the morning?"

"My father sent me to the big pasture just over the next hill to relieve my brother. Our sheep are lambing," the boy explained.

"Is your brother older than you?" she asked.

"Yes, he is sixteen. He has been out here alone since midnight." The lad studied the girl's face for a moment. "Miss," he said, showing real concern, "would you like to get on my horse behind me? I can take you to San Angelo. My brother won't mind waiting."

Catherine thanked the boy graciously as he jumped to the ground to help her.

Inside the convent the two sisters met in fond embrace as Clare gave way to tears of gratitude. "I knew that you would come, Catherine," she said fervently. "Soon we will have a place to call our own where we shall receive girls whose dedication to God shall equal our own and that of the *Fratres Minores*. I can hardly wait."

"Nor I, Clare," said her sister. "From the time you left us I have dreamed of this moment when we would be together again."

"What about Monaldo and the men?" asked Clare. "They will be coming for you no later than this very morning or I miss my guess. Are you willing to face them?"

"Yes, Clare," she answered. "I shall face them alone. Everyone is afraid of Monaldo unless it would be Cousin Ruffino. He refused to go along to Saint Paul's when they tried to bring you back."

"Poor, dear Ruffino," said Clare. "He is always so somber and serious. Did you know that he never misses a chance to hear Francis preach? I saw him every time, standing alone in the shadows, hoping I think that none of the family would notice him."

"Wouldn't it be wonderful if he were converted?" said Catherine. "We must remember him in our prayers."

The two sisters spent the morning together, planning, praying, reminiscing. Then, just before noon—while sitting together in the garden—they heard the hoofs of several horses and guessed correctly that Monaldo and his nephews had found them.

"Face them boldly," said Clare. "I shall go inside and watch from a window. If you need me I shall come. Surely the two of us can convince them that you too have given your life to God." She hurried away.

Catherine stood with her back against a tree watching Monaldo and three of her cousins dismount at the gate, fifteen rods down the hill from the garden. To her great surprise she recognized Ruffino who stayed with the horses as the others made their way quickly between thorny shrubs and scrub cedars to the terrace. Monaldo was in no mood to beg. When he saw calm defiance written on Catherine's countenance, he lost control completely. Before anyone realized what was happening, he leaped forward, grabbed the girl's wrist, and began dragging her down the hill. The young men followed in angry amazement. When they saw thorns tearing their cousin's clothing and flesh—blood flowing from deep scratches on her legs—they screamed their protests, but Monaldo paid no attention. Clare, hardly able to believe her eyes, came running from the house crying for help. Monaldo, intent upon his gruesome task, fixed his eyes upon the ground lest his own feet should stumble, and failed to notice Ruffino sprinting up the hill to meet him. With one gigantic leap the young man tackled his uncle around the neck and slapped him to the ground. The half-crazed man pulled himself up to face three irate nephews and Clare as Catherine came to her feet.

"I hope you're satisfied," said Clare as Monaldo watched the younger girl limp away slowly.

Aware that he had lost another battle, the unhappy man turned his back upon the others to mount his horse and gallop off toward town.

"Thank you, Ruffino," said Clare softly. "It was wonderfully brave of you to oppose our uncle. He will not be easy for you to live with, we may be sure."

"It doesn't matter," answered Ruffino. "For some time the Lord has been speaking to my heart. I am going now to Francis and his men; if they will have me I shall become a Lesser Brother.

17

The Third Order

Francis was sitting in quiet meditation when Ruffino approached Saint Mary's of the Angels at the Little Portion. The sun was low in the western sky. The evangelist was both grateful and amused as he listened to the story of the day's events from the somber relative of the two girls who had accomplished their final break with the world. Ruffino was embarrassed as he tried to describe his own part in the fracas which was so out of character with his serious, often melancholy spirit. Francis smiled broadly for an instant then became the personification of solemnity.

"Ruffino," he said, "tell me about yourself. I have known for weeks that the Spirit of our blessed Lord has been dogging your steps."

"Yes, Francis. He has become most precious to my soul. If only I were worthy of His love, I would ask to be numbered among your faithful disciples."

"No one deserves His love, Ruffino," said Francis softly. "All have sinned and fallen far, far short of His glory. But He has provided grace, free and sufficient, for our salvation. I must warn you, though, that the way we take is not easy. One's commitment to God must be complete—without reservation—or the path would be intolerable."

"I understand," said the candidate.

Then Francis recited the Primitive Rule with appropriate comments.

"I have counted the cost," answered Ruffino simply. "I want nothing but the will of God and a small corner of His vineyard in which to labor."

So it happened that the first male member of Clare's noble family became one of the most dedicated and loyal of all the Franciscans.

"Tomorrow," said Francis, "I want you to go with me to talk with Bishop Guido regarding a convent for the new order for women which will be established soon with the help of God. It may be that the bishop will want to hear firsthand of Monaldo's humiliating defeat."

But the humble man declined. "I must grow in grace and knowledge," he said simply. "Please excuse me so that I may give my time to prayer."

At the bishop's place, Francis learned from Guido that his old friend, Peter of San Damiano, had suffered a stroke.

"We must visit him at once," said the bishop. "I was told that he was asking for you when he awoke this morning."

When the two men arrived at his bedside, Peter tried to raise his head. "My boy, my boy," he wheezed as he turned his eyes to Francis. "I knew that you would come. Listen carefully for I haven't much time left, as you can see. Do you remember how the Lord made plain to you one day that San Damiano would become a monastery for females of holy life?"

"Yes, Father," the young man answered.

"Go, Francis, find out who holds the rights to the property now, and make known my dying wish that Clare and her loyal friends might be cloistered here to serve the Lord with gladness." The dying man seemed unaware that Bishop

Guido was in the room also.

"Ah, Peter," spoke the bishop quickly, "Francis need not go away to get his information. Many months ago I came into full possession of San Damiano, and you may be sure that I shall gladly turn it over for such a noble purpose."

Then the faithful Peter closed his tired eyes and smiled. Less than an hour later, with Francis at his side, he rallied for a moment, tried to speak, then crossed quietly the border-line of worlds.

Francis wept.

In the days that followed, the Lesser Brothers, under Francis' direction, completely renovated the premises at San Damiano in preparation for Clare and Catherine to take residence and receive their first recruits. (The new order was called the Poor Clares, and Catherine took the name of Sister Agnes.)

Back at the Little Portion Francis called the brothers together for consultation. "The time has come," he said quietly, "to establish a third order for converts—men and women—who obviously can join neither the Lesser Brothers nor the Poor Clares but who have come to love the Lord. Where do you men propose that we begin?"

It was Giles who finally broke the silence. "What about the rancher and his wife who live up the trail toward Gubbio whose little boy wants to join us when he is older?"

"Good," said Francis. "I have been thinking of them today. Giles, since you are acquainted with the family, go and ask them to meet us here tomorrow afternoon. Let us all go now to bring in as many of our converts as we can, and we shall give them a rule and establish their order."

By noon the following day the people were arriving at the Little Portion. Fathers, mothers, entire families—large and small—farmers, merchants, tradesmen—young and old—poured in from every direction. When Giles returned with the herdsman and his little family there was another couple in the party: Jacob and Maria di Arezzo with whom Francis had stayed in Gubbio. They came running to their old friend. Maria's round face was aglow as she told Francis of their conversion which came about soon after he left their household. "We could never be the same again," she told him. "We were on our way to visit you when we met Brother Giles. We didn't know him, of course, but when we mentioned your name he invited us to come along with him and this precious family from the little sheep ranch. Surely God is smiling upon us all today."

The revival rolled on with two ministries being mightily used by God: *mass evangelism* with some of the men—Francis in particular—preaching to unprecedented crowds wherever they went and *personal evangelism* with all the men—Giles in particular—presenting the claims of Christ to the twos and threes wherever they found them. A new convert, of course, was allowed to choose the order which best met his need, and all three orders grew with amazing swiftness. Soon the Franciscans, numbering far into the thousands, could no longer be counted because chapters were moving across Italy and even beyond.

The "Chapter General" was initiated as an annual event at which time the Lesser Brothers would convene at the Little Portion for fellowship and instruction. It was Francis' way of maintaining unity and forestalling any serious deviation from the rule by which they lived and died. It was not long until more than five thousand loyal brothers, dressed in their tunics of sackcloth, converged upon Assisi every year to share their victories and discuss their problems.

At the close of each chapter Francis retired to a lonely hermitage far up the mountain to fast and pray—petitioning heaven for necessary strength and wisdom to carry his awesome responsibility. Then he would return to the Little Portion, renewed in spirit, mind, and body, rejoicing always, praying ceaselessly, giving thanks in all things, honoring the Spirit, and, above all, avoiding the appearance of evil.

At San Damiano, Clare was loaded with the cares of a growing community of sisters who lived together closely, for in thirteenth-century Italy nuns were strictly cloistered. On one occasion of Francis' return from his favorite hideout a messenger awaited him. Clare wanted to know whether it was possible for her to have dinner with Francis—strictly chaperoned—so that they might discuss important matters and break the loneliness of life within monastic walls.

Francis consented. He was aware that a bit of diversion would be most beneficial to the faithful Clare, so he arranged to have her brought to the Little Portion where a banquet table of plain boards was set just outside Saint Mary's of the Angels. How he negotiated her exit from the convent has been an unsolved riddle for more than seven centuries, but nonetheless he did it. He was a saint.

When the party was seated and the meager fare served, Francis—overflowing with joy from his recent seclusion with God—began to talk of spiritual things engendering a visitation of the Spirit upon all who were present. Faces were aglow, tears unrestrained, and spiritual food was served in such abundance that the provisions for the physical man were left untouched.

Giles said later that God was pleased to place another stamp of approval upon the Franciscans and, in His wisdom, chose a time when all three orders were represented.

18

Beautiful Feet

The church in the first century was missionary minded, carrying the gospel over mountains and seas to heathen lands; but, during the Dark Ages, its last tiny spark of zeal to evangelize the pagan—especially on foreign soil—was snuffed out in the wake of religious warfare. The awful truth of this broke in upon Francis' open mind during a fast in the mountains. In that moment, even as the ill-fated Children's Crusade was getting underway—the year was 1212—God was pleased to kindle again the fire of missionary passion, and chose for it the pure heart of Francis of Assisi. But one is made to shudder when he thinks how close the thirty-year-old evangelist came to missing the message completely.

Francis had never been quick to grasp divine orders. His conversion, like his acceptance of Lady Poverty and his comprehension of God's call, had been slow in developing; but, once the light broke through, he never failed to stand foursquare by his convictions. Recently he had received what he believed was a mandate from heaven to launch out into some greater area of service, but he was without a single clue as to what that might involve. Then, as always, the answer came.

One morning, in his search for divine direction, Francis called a small group of his friars together at the Little Portion.

"Brothers," he said, "I am leaving you this morning, for I must get alone to fast and pray. It seems that God has new plans for us; I shall give Him every opportunity to reveal His will—"

The little speech was interrupted by Brother Ruffino.

"Father," he said quickly, knowing that when Francis finished his exhortation he would be on his way, "last night a brother from France arrived in Assisi. He speaks only his native tongue and wishes to talk with you."

Francis was delighted. For years he had wanted to visit his mother's homeland, and French was his favorite language.

"Present this brother at once, Ruffino," he commanded kindly.

In a few moments a young man, thin, wiry, and travel worn, with black eyes, olive skin, and sensitive mouth made his appearance. Francis saw that this was no ordinary fellow.

"Welcome to the Little Portion." Francis spoke in the dialect of the troubadours. "Please, what is your name?"

"Call me André," he answered.

"I understand that you have just come from France, André. Tell us about it."

"My home is Paris," the young man explained, "but just now I have come from Spain, and I bring disturbing news."

"Go on," said Francis.

"A brother named Paula and I left home four months ago to see if God would help us revive His church in Spain," began André. "We ran into war. Christians equipped with the finest armor, shields, and weapons charged from the south and plowed through the ranks of the savage Moors in the bloodiest battle I think the world has ever seen. We were captured by a small group of Moors, and Paula spoke to them of Christ and His kingdom. He was put to death right before my eyes." The young man paused in an effort to control his emotions. "Paula is with the martyrs, Father," he continued. "I would be too if I were not a coward. I escaped and ran two days before stopping to beg for food and a place to rest. I stayed another day to work in the fields to pay for my keep before going to the coast. I was given work on a boat that took me to Naples; then I made my way to Rome and Assisi."

"Has the war in Spain ended?" asked Francis.

"I think so," answered André. "It is supposed to be a great victory for the church."

Francis was silent. From his childhood he had been taught that the church waged holy wars—the Crusades, for instance—that were used by God to defeat His enemies and establish His kingdom.

"Should we not rejoice?" he asked seriously. "Is it not well that the heathen's power has been broken?"

"I'm not sure, Father." André, sensing his immaturity, was moving with caution. "That is why I am disturbed."

During the pause that followed, this extremely young man must have felt that he faced the king and his court. He had to decide quickly whether it was expedient for him to voice his convictions. He was tempted, as all intelligent men are, to hold his tongue; but he felt strongly—his convictions were deeply ingrained—and he had come a long way for the single purpose of delivering his soul.

Francis sensed a dilemma. "You are among friends, André," he said simply. "Do not be afraid to speak your mind. That is the way of the Lesser Brothers."

So André spoke, cutting through to the heart of the problem as the young are prone to do. "Surely it is right that we of the Primitive Rule follow Christ without purse or scrip or even a beggar's bag," he stated firmly. "Can we expect Him then to honor Christians who carry armor, spears, and crossbows to usher into hell the souls of men who have never heard His promise of salvation?"

Francis pondered the question for many long moments. "I had a friend once whose name was Gallo," he said thoughtfully. "He would have liked you very much. When I was a boy the Lord was pleased to use him to open my heart and mind to truth."

The men were strangely silent as Francis studied his new friend carefully. "Perhaps, André," he went on, "God didn't want you to occupy a martyr's seat in paradise—not yet at least—that you might come today to enlighten me further. I shall see you when I return."

Francis paused long enough to speak a blessing of peace upon his fellows, then made his way up the lonely trail to find his rendezvous with God.

Two days later he returned to the Little Portion with a new sermon.

"With love—not hate—the church must bring the pagan to his knees," he told the brothers who sat in a half-circle at his feet. "We shall be crusaders too and penetrate the distant lands."

"We shall go unarmed, of course," voiced Peter of Catanei.

"No," said Francis quickly. "Our witness shall be the most powerful crossbow the world has ever seen. Our arrows will be tipped with barbs of truth. We shall destroy our enemies forever by making them brothers in the Lord."

André sprang to his feet to grasp Francis in his embrace, then begged permission to leave at once to take the gospel to the Moors.

As André left the Little Portion, headed back toward Spain, Francis turned to the brothers to ask whether there were questions. After an exceptionally long pause, Brother Elias, an aggressive leader among the friars in whom Francis had come to place strong confidence, arose to present a problem.

"Father," he said with profound respect, "your words

will not be taken lightly. You have opened our minds and blessed our hearts. All of us will cherish the day when we can penetrate the darkness of heathen nations to follow your instructions."

"Thank you," said Francis, "but I sense that something immediate is bothering you."

"Yes," answered the friar, "we face a serious situation involving the pagan at our own doorstep which we do not know how to handle."

"Please explain," said the other.

"In the woods, not far from here, there resides a band of robbers," said Elias. "Recently the leader has been sending one or two of his crafty fellows to the Little Portion, demanding that we give them food. We do not know whether it is right to refuse anyone who is hungry or wrong to give food to strengthen bandits to pursue their evil ways."

"What has been your response to their appeals?" asked Francis.

"Sometimes we give them food," the friar answered. "When we are short on rations, we refuse them."

"What is your motive when you grant their demands?" Francis probed. "Why do you give them food?"

"Because, Father," Elias anwered honestly, "we are afraid they will call their fellows and take everything."

"And what is your reason for refusing to share with them the little you have on other occasions?" He probed deeper.

"We feel certain that they will not raid our pantry when we have little more than nothing for them to steal." Elias was aware that these were weak answers. So, in an effort at vindication he said, "We justify our refusal to divide with them for the reason that they are thieves."

"Either road you travel is a wrong one!" spoke the leader sternly.

"Yes, Father, we know," Elias answered weakly, "but still we don't know what to do."

"Listen carefully," instructed Francis. "One who is unable or unwilling to take Christ to the pagan just beyond his own doorstep is neither worthy nor capable of taking Him to the far side of rugged mountains or over distant seas."

It was apparent that the little evangelist meant exactly what he was saying, and every brother gave strict attention.

"Take some loaves and wine," he continued, "and go into the woods in search of the robbers. Cry out to the evil fellows! In the name of Christ offer them provisions for which they will have neither begged nor tried to steal. When they have had their fill they will be in a proper mood to listen to your witness. Don't preach; tell them simply of the wonderful life you live with Christ as your captain, and virture your ideal. And when you leave, admonish the culprits to behave themselves, promising to see them again."

"Then what?" the brothers cried in unison.

"Wait two days," continued Francis, "and go back with more loaves and wine, adding hard-cooked eggs and fruit to the fare. Present the claims of Christ, explaining redemption and lead them to the Cross. Some of them will become good *Fratres Minores;* the rest will leave, never to bother you again."

The brothers did as they were told, and more than half the robber gang were soon converted.

Then, in further effort "to earn their spurs" the happy friars set out by twos again to make short missionary journeys over much the same ground they had traveled before. This time they directed their message to infidels rather than to the wayward sons of the church.

Francis always gave the best advice to his men but failed often to keep his own counsel, which may have been the case regarding his own first foreign missionary tour, for his plans failed utterly. He was certain that the infidels in Syria needed converting, a fact which seemed incentive enough for him to enlist the company of Brother Leo, his secretary, and proceed to make the journey. So the two men set sail from Ancona, but soon a storm arose with which the boat's crew of hardy sailors fought for days and nights as Francis and his friend, like the Apostle Paul, expected never to see the sun again. Then ironically, on the same day that the sun smiled down through the clouds once more, the sturdy craft was wrecked forever on the rocks of Dalmatia. Not a life was lost, however. The rough, drenched seamen stood safely on *terra firma,* cursing Jupiter and every other god on land and sea while they watched the angry waters lash the shore. But Francis and Leo sang praises unto heaven, then asked the men to build a fire, for they were going out in search of food.

"Curse Jove if you must," said Francis, "but remember that the God of David heard our prayers and saved our lives."

A blazing, crackling fire was sending sparks high into the night when the brothers returned laden with provisions. When stomachs were full and spirits lifted, the men gathered in a half-circle around the fire as Francis and Leo proceeded naturally enough to evangelize them. Two of the men responded to the gospel to experience the joy of salvation; the others, as would be expected, sneaked away in the darkness of the night.

By morning the winds had receded, and boats appeared once more upon the horizon. Then the four men left their little camp to follow the shoreline and came finally to a tiny port where a ship was about to head back toward Italy. But Francis and his friends were penniless, and the ship's captain, who had just weathered the murderous tumult, was in no mood to be accommodating. The two recently converted seamen, however, were offered jobs on the boat which they quickly accepted. They gave Francis and Leo the food and water they carried from the camp and advised the brothers to go aboard in the night and hide beneath a pile of canvas that was stored below.

Leo was hesitant. "It is wrong to steal a ride," he said gloomily.

"I know what you mean," said Francis, "but I have a feeling that we may be needed on this journey. Since our passage will neither cost nor inconvenience anyone, perhaps the Lord will not object."

Right or wrong, the brothers were stowaways when the ship put out to sea. Francis' feeling that he and Leo might be needed may well have been a premonition, for in the night the storm returned with all its former fury. To keep the boat from being dashed to pieces, the crew

143

expertly negotiated every swell as they steered for open waters.

Francis and Leo, still in hiding, were sadly afflicted with the ancient sickness of the deep. The result was that, when the seas were finally calm again, they had not touched one crumb of their provisions, while the crew, needing more than ordinary strength for their battle with the elements, had bolted every scrap of food and gulped down the last drop of water in the galley. They were yet two days from the port of Ancona, nearly mad with thirst and hunger. Then it was that two little men in brown tunics of sackcloth appeared upon the deck with ample provisions for all.

That evening Francis had no difficulty calling the men together for preaching, after which Leo and the two converted seamen arose to tell of the grace of God that reached their hearts and gave them peace.

"Repent," they said, "the kingdom of God is at hand!"

Strangely enough, it was the tough old captain who was first to confess his sins.

While Francis and Leo were away, some of the brothers returned to the Little Portion. From a human standpoint, the missionary movement was off to such a poor start that most of the men voiced their discouragement and lamented their failure, until Bernard di Quintavalle arose to defend the new ministry.

"Brothers," he said, "we are mistaking the pains of birth for the groans of death. A new movement is being born. Francis will be returning soon, and we shall ask his permission to visit every nation under heaven. We will be persecuted. Many, no doubt, will join the martyrs in paradise, but Christ and His kingdom shall be exalted, for we will have gone into all the world with the gospel." Then, quoting from the sacred writings, he continued, *"How beautiful are the feet of them that preach the gospel of peace and bring glad tidings of good things."*

"Bernard is right," spoke up Sylvester. "We shall go and never stop, for 'how shall they hear without a preacher?' "

19

La Verna

Francis and Leo made their way slowly back to Assisi.
They followed no direct route, stopped in every hamlet,
preached to the poor, and ministered to the lepers as they
sang, witnessed, and finally climbed a steep mountain
to an obscure hermitage to fast and pray. As they were
leaving their place of seclusion, Francis paused to gaze
upward toward the towering peak.

"Brother Leo," he said with fervor, "somewhere the
Lord has such an eminence as this that He would be
pleased to give to the Lesser Brothers.

"Once the Little Portion and Rivo-Torto were all we
needed, but now our numbers have grown until we have
no place to retreat for meditation. Let us pray that such
a majestic mountain as this one will be made available
to us."

Leo, who always took notes of his leader's words

and wishes, was so certain that Francis' utterance was prophetic that he wrote it down as if the request were already granted. And when the two men reached Assisi, Leo told Sylvester that God was providing the *Fratres Minores* with a great snow-crested mountain for their very own. "There, with Father Francis," he said, "we will fast and pray as we formulate our plans to go into all the world and preach the gospel."

Sylvester was delighted. "Where is this paradise?" he asked.

Leo, gazing toward a bank of billowy clouds in the east, spoke as one in a dream. "At this point," he said, "no one knows but God. But it will come."

And Sylvester believed it too—believed it so strongly that he helped spread the news to all the brethren.

In the autumn of 1212, Francis made a trip to Rome to report the progress of the *Fratres Minores* to Pope Innocent. It was he who had said, "Come back, my brothers, when your numbers have multiplied, and further favors will be granted you, and greater missions entrusted to your care."

The pope, deeply impressed by the unprecedented spread of the revival, listened closely to every detail of Francis' report. Most amazing was the effect (or the lack of it) of so successful a ministry upon Francis. The pope understood people—the frailties of human nature were hardly strangers to a man of his experience—so naturally he studied Francis with this in mind. Normally, so successful a leader would have changed greatly by this time, but not Francis. He was dressed in the original brown sackcloth, expressed the same simple faith in God and asked no favor except the freedom to preach repentance to the pagan as well as to the backslidden sons of the church. But—and Francis made plain one stipulation—there must be no geographical nor cultural limits placed upon the ministry. The gospel was for all men everywhere.

The pontiff conceded, and Francis returned to Assisi, where through the winter of 1212-1213 he ministered to the lepers in their little huts at a hospital just outside the city.

During the Lenten season that spring a late storm blanketed all Italy with snow. The mountains to the north were buried many feet beneath the cold, white cover, and temperatures dropped to a record low. Then, as often happens when summer prepares to make its approach, warm winds moved in causing every creek and river to overflow its banks and flood the countryside.

Francis was impatient, as ambitious men in springtime always are. By the last of April all was clear; snowcapped mountains smiled down upon the fields and pastures which were turning green, and the *Fratres Minores* went everywhere singing psalms of praise, witnessing, begging, and working.

So it happened—providentially, no doubt—that Francis and Leo made a journey into a magnificent wonderland of the Apennines. Walking along the rugged terrain one day, they came suddenly in view of a castle high above their heads that belonged to Count Orlando di Catanei, a wealthy nobleman with a reputation for his piety, pride, and generosity. There was music and laughter for this day a youthful cousin of Orlando's was being initiated into the sublime mysteries of knighthood, and a festival appropriate for the occasion was being given by the wealthy count. The brothers listened for a while to the music and applause of the happy throng, then moved noiselessly up the stone steps to stand in the shadows and watch the festivities.

Francis found it hard to take his eyes off a young man who, that morning, following the singing of the mass, had received his spurs. To become a knight had once been his own chief ambition. But it would not be fair to leave the impression that Francis felt sorry for himself or coveted in the least the young man's honor. He was wed to Poverty without a hint of reservation. His one desire now was to preach Christ crucified and risen to Orlando and his guests. Soon his opportunity came, for one of the guards discovered the two friars and recognized the celebrated evangelist whose fame was sweeping all of Europe.

"A sermon, please," the great crowd chanted.

Francis needed no other invitation.

He preached with divine unction, carrying the throng to unprecedented heights of ecstasy with magnificent peals of oratory. As he closed, his last words echoed in the court before melting into the awesome silence that reigned supreme over the medieval castle.

Then Count Orlando himself came forward to ask the friars to help him find the peace and joy of salvation.

"Of course," said Francis, "but you must not be rude to your guests. Go dine with them. When you have cared properly for your responsibilities, we will find a quiet place to discuss your spiritual need and talk with God."

Orlando so appreciated this display of thoughtfulness that after the counseling session—filled with the peace that passes all understanding—he told the evangelist that he wished to make him a present.

"I own thousands of acres in these mountains," he said simply. "Do you see among those snowcapped peaks the one that stands out more beautiful than all his fellows? That one we call La Verna." The count paused for a moment to be sure that Francis was following him. "I am giving La Verna to you and to your *Fratres Minores,*" he continued. "I believe the Lord will be pleased when you accept it and use it to His glory."

20

Pray, Preach, or Die

To Francis, all creation—animal, vegetable, mineral—had a common father in God. Hence, every man, bird, rock, and tree were brothers and sisters in a very real sense. He was kind to his brother, the worm, as he picked him up and placed him beside the path; he preached to his sisters, the birds; he practiced patience with all men; and he loved all of nature. Then he became cruel in his treatment of himself. He considered his body a brother to his soul but referred to it as a braying ass. He was known to deal severely with his men who sought favor from heaven through self-imposed suffering, but he demanded too much of his own body through excessive travel, preaching, praying, fasting, counseling, healing, and generally relieving suffering in an all-out effort to fulfill his call from God.

Now for the first time he sensed that he was growing

weary and longed for peace and rest. His oldest friend, Bernard di Quintavalle, who by this time had established a community of Lesser Brothers in Bologna, had warned him of the dangers he faced in continuing the pace he had long pursued.

Pray, preach, or die—what should he do? There was never a moment that he would not have welcomed a martyr's death if God had seen fit to allow it, but he always came through the most dangerous assignments. When the body is weak, however, temptation grows strong. To preach was his call, but now that the revival had spread beyond his wildest dreams, he tended to rationalize—to convince himself that he had accomplished his mission. This, he contended with delight, left him free to retire to La Verna where he could give the remainder of his life to adoration, praise, and intercession, reveling in the presence of the Christ.

But Francis was practical enough to fear that the message might be coming through from "Brother Body" rather than from "Father God." If so, it was probably at the instigation of the devil. He longed for the godly counsel of his old friend, Peter of San Damiano.

He was groaning beneath the burden of indecision when he and Leo came tramping through the woods to the Little Portion following their extraordinary experience with Count Orlando.

"Where have you been?" the brothers asked.

"Tell them," said Francis, "and, of course, you will not forget to mention the gift that we received."

"I can guess," spoke up Sylvester. "You have been given a mountain."

"Yes, Sylvester," Leo answered. "Count Orlando was converted when Francis preached at the castle, after which he gave the Lesser Brothers Mount La Verna, the most beautiful spot in all that part of the Apennines."

After a season of rejoicing, Leo continued his report and Francis arose to address the brethren.

"Brothers," he said, "I need your prayers. For the first time in my life I am growing weary of the road. If it would please God I would like to retire to a hermitage and give the remainder of my life to prayer, interceding for the

Lesser Brothers and groaning for peace to reign over these war-cursed nations of the earth. I am most anxious for your reaction."

"What about our mission to carry the gospel to the far corners of the world?" asked Ruffino.

"Those plans will not be altered at all," Francis explained carefully. "I am planning to appoint a successor to take leadership of our order in the near future anyway. The only change will be in my own way of life."

"Father," spoke up Peter of Catanei, "we will need to give your suggestion much thought and prayer. This is not the time for a hasty decision."

The summer wore on. The chapter general that year was the greatest ever—the order was growing on every front—but nothing seemed to alter Francis' thinking regarding his retirement.

The brothers became fearful that some disease was fastening itself upon his lean body. Since he was still in his early thirties, he should have been at the peak of his strength, charging forward with his men.

It was true that he no longer had the resistance necessary to fight off the germs of disease—germs of which men of that century were blissfully unaware. Of course, it is impossible to diagnose an illness of seven centuries ago. But one may well guess that Francis, even then, was moving into the initial stages of tuberculosis, and if it had not been for the rugged out-of-door life he lived, the malady might have closed in upon him with much greater rapidity. Francis, who was strangely naive in some areas, was never overly burdened with worries, a fact which probably helped him retain a measure of health for an extended period. For instance, it was impossible for him to accept the fact that men of liberal tendencies were beginning to infiltrate the order of the *Fratres Minores*—but it was true. Even then there were those who were advocating the construction of luxurious dormitories to replace the huts and dugouts in which the men had always found refuge and rest. They wanted to generally update the organization that it might take its place beside the many older and more sophisticated orders within the church. When he was told that one of his most trusted, talented friars, Brother Elias, was a leader behind the scenes in the movement to liberalize the Franciscans, he refused to listen to another word.

At the chapter general of 1214, Brother André, the young missionary to the Moors in Spain, appeared again at the Little Portion. Francis could hardly have been more pleased. He set up immediately a three o'clock in the morning appointment with him in the tiny chapel, Saint Mary's of the Angels. They were most likely to be undisturbed at this early hour. This meeting, which lasted until sunup, may have changed the course of Francis' later years.

With delight, he listened as André talked without embarrassment of his successful missionary efforts in Spain, while admitting that he was in nowise satisfied with his accomplishments. André had a way of turning the conversation toward the future and his projected plans—plans which, in every instance, paralleled the promises of God. Francis recognized in all of this the essence of pure humility and wondered, as the ultra-conscientious are prone to do, whether sinful pride had not invaded his own heart upon occasion.

"Pray for me, André," said Francis seriously. "It is my great desire, with the help of God, to maintain complete fidelity to my Lady Poverty."

"I will, of course," answered André. "And I covet your own petitions in my behalf, that I shall never give the appearance of being less obedient to heaven than the heretics who are making great strides against us."

"Do you refer to the Albigenses?" Francis asked.

"Yes," said André. "For years they have preached their doctrines in southern France, and every effort of the church to destroy them has failed. Now they have moved into Spain. The problem is that these heretics live carefully disciplined lives even as we do. It is hard for the converted Moors to understand why we do not work together."

"One must appreciate the fact that they live well," said Francis, "for there are those within the church who don't."

"I know," said André. "I have dwelt many times upon such thoughts as that, but there are two elements in their preaching that tend to nauseate me. The first is an everlasting bragging of their virtues; and second, the greater part of their every message is a loud tirade against the church. There is moral corruption among them too, but in an effort to keep their skirts clean, they expell forever those who are found guilty. There is no forgiveness."

"Are many expelled?" asked Francis.

"One of their leaders told me," answered André, "that every year the number increases until it becomes a serious problem with them."

"I think I understand," said Francis thoughtfully. "A long time ago Peter of San Damiano warned me of the dangers I would face within my own order. 'Beware,' he said, 'of the brother who makes a show of being more holy than his fellows.' And on another occasion he suggested that I watch closely a friar who preaches too often on any *one* of the virtues. 'For instance,' he said, 'if the overworked subject happens to be *chastity,* it will be well to follow the brother some night and see where he goes.' "

"Do you know Dominic Gusmann?" asked André. "He is doing his best to win the Albigenses. I enjoy wonderful fellowship with him and his men. It seems that this learned, godly man once asked permission of the pope to carry the gospel to the barbarians in central Europe—especially Hungary—but was ordered rather to stem the heresy in southwestern France. Dominic," André went on, "with all his culture, training, and position of prominence in the bishop's cabinet, has discovered the power of poverty even as we have."

"Is he a young man?" asked Francis.

"No," answered André thoughtfully, "I would presume that he is ten years your senior, maybe more. He makes a fine appearance, dresses immaculately in clerical garb of black, but his humility and dedication are immediately recognizable. I wish you could meet him. His men call themselves the Preaching Brothers, but they have not received permission to establish an order. Dominic says

153

he believes Pope Innocent would admit them, but the cardinals object. It is supposed that there are already too many orders within the church, so the Dominicans should join one of the others. I wish you could meet him."

"I will meet him," answered Francis slowly.

When the chapter general ended, Francis found himself surrounded once more by a lingering group of his special friends. "Brothers," he said, "I must make my decision at once. Shall I give the remainder of my life to preaching or to prayer? I have been thinking of Brother Sylvester. He was a selfish priest who sought and accepted the cross in great humility to become an apostle of intercession. Now his prayers are coveted by all the brothers. I wish too that I might hear Sister Clare repeat the words she spoke to me when she was twelve years old: "I have said prayers for you every day for years. You may be sure I shall continue."

He turned then to Brother Masseo. "Go," he said, "and present my problem to Brother Sylvester and Sister Clare. When they have prayed and believe they have the mind of the Lord, bring me their answers. If they agree, I shall accept their verdict as the voice of God."

Masseo did as he was told, returning two days later. Francis' faith in the prayers of his friends was such that he considered this one of the great hours of his life and arranged a fitting ceremony in which to receive so important a revelation as he believed was forthcoming. The decision was unanimous. *Sylvester and Clare were agreed that Francis should continue to preach, for there were yet untold victories to gain.*

Thus came an end to his indecision and with it a marvelous uplift of spirit. His health even, so the brothers noted, seemed wonderfully improved.

21

And in Samaria

In the months that followed, Francis gave himself without reservation to evangelistic preaching. Crowds, greater than ever, gathered in every instance as the revival itself experienced a powerful renewal.

Not only were the people moved to seek the peace of God for themselves, but all were made aware of their responsibility as believers to promote spiritual rather than military victory over the Moslems, infidels, barbarians, and heretics everywhere. Youthful converts felt a special call to missionary service and pleaded with Francis to send them to the far frontiers of the thirteenth-century world.

"In God's time you shall go," Francis told them. "We have been promised power to witness effectively, first 'in Jerusalem and in all Judea' (Assisi and all Italy); 'and in Samaria' (the nations of Europe that join us);

'and even to the remotest part of the earth.' "

During the summer of 1215, Francis made another trip to Rome; the burden of his missionary enterprise was heavy upon his heart. It was there that he met Dominic Gusmann, who later became the founder of the Order of Dominicans. The two men so different in background, training, and appearance were strangely alike in heart and ambition. Both men, as leaders in spiritual revival, were highly respected by bishops, cardinals, and especially the pope. There was little doubt that Innocent III, who had waged some of the bloodiest wars in history, saw in his declining years that the only real and lasting answer to the problems confronting the kingdom of God were to be found in the message of peace.

It was at this time that the pope inaugurated the Lateran Council which strongly opposed the establishing of new orders within the church. Hence, Dominic, who was a full-fledged priest, was refused recognition again. He accepted, as second best, permission to develop his work under an ancient rule of Saint Augustine.

But an exception was made in the case of Francis and the Lesser Brothers, a fact which forever documents the personality and power of the little lay evangelist. It is true that Francis, by this time, had received deacon's orders which must have been—as we might say today—an honorary rather than an earned "degree." While he was naturally intelligent he was not a student, and he even refused his friars the luxury of owning books. To pursue formal education, he contended, would rob one of his deep spirituality, an error which still invades the church sometimes. But—and this is the miracle—it was over this error that Francis rode to victory, where Dominic failed.

Pope Innocent III died in midsummer 1216 with Francis at his side. He was succeeded by the elderly Honorius III, who also held Francis and the Lesser Brothers in high esteem. As the Cardinal of San Sabina had befriended Francis in an earlier situation, so now did a future pontiff, Cardinal Ugolino, take the Franciscans under his wing.

Cardinal Ugolino was well aware that the simple faith and wholly dedicated lives of the Lesser Brothers was just the leaven needed to permeate the whole loaf—to put new spiritual life into every area of the church. But Ugolino was an experienced churchman—a cardinal—and hardly deaf to a whispering among his colleagues that one day they would probably be casting their ballots in his favor to ascend the papal throne. So, important also in his thinking was the hierarchy, the prestige and power of office, and the talent and preparation necessary for one to rise from the ranks. In short, Ugolino was a sincere man of faith, and at the same time, a polished politician. To him, the future success—or existence, even—of the *Fratres Minores* was contingent upon their discarding the literal interpretation of the Primitive Rule, and rising to a place of prominence in the church, taking with them their deep spirituality, of course. Eventually there should be Franciscan bishops, Franciscan cardinals, and, far in the future perhaps, but why not some day a Franciscan pope?

It is hard for men who are politically ambitious to realize that there are others beneath them who have no desire for the power and prestige of office. Hence, it is understandable that Ugolino found it difficult to comprehend Francis' abhorrence of his suggestions. And the little evangelist was amazed at the cardinal's inability to see that the spirit and practice of absolute poverty alone was necessary to the success of his movement. For a *Frater Minor* to become a *Frater Major* would be to turn his back upon the power which, through the Lesser Brothers, had already shaken the Catholic world. And it was the freedom derived from this same power that made it possible for Francis to stand completely unafraid before the mighty churchman and openly oppose his plan. Francis of Assisi was running neither *for* nor *from* anything.

And Cardinal Ugolino, like Pope Innocent on an earlier occasion, could find no argument with which to defend his case against the scriptural rule that led the *Fratres Minores*—now numbering in multiplied thousands—down a narrow road of unprecedented achievement. He backed down. No doubt he had been enlightened, for he continued to champion the cause of the Franciscans, and kept the strange order of humble friars beneath his protecting wing throughout his life.

So, when the chapter general of 1217 decided that the time had come for the brothers to penetrate the nations of Europe with the gospel—even without such elementary preparation as language study—Ugolino, against his better judgment, conceded.

The men moved out immediately in many directions with no less than fifty friars traveling northward into Germany. It was from there the feudal lords had come to rule Italian communities from stark medieval castles, and—after their crushing defeat of 1198—it was to Germany they had fled again. It was hostile territory; even the German Catholics considered the strange men in their patched brown tunics some kind of heretics. Great was the persecution; devastating was the cold and hunger; and generally unsuccessful were the reports of the friars who dared invade the Germans. And equally unsuccessful were the other missionary bands on their first journeys into "Samaria" with the gospel. Militating in their favor was the one fact that the revival which began in Assisi had reached into every one of these bordering nations. The problem was that it took time for the people to properly associate the awakening with the humble preachers who now came singing down their roads.

But the brothers benefited greatly by the experiment, learning that perseverance must always be found in a missionary's tool chest; and preparation, especially through language study and an understanding of the culture of the peoples invaded, ought never to be neglected either.

Francis, of course, could not now stand idly by while others faced the hardships of the road, so he too planned a journey across national boundaries, remembering that his first such trip—a boat ride to Syria—was never completed. Where would he go? For years he had hoped that someday he might visit his mother's homeland, so now he asked the Lord whether He would be pleased to have His humble servant go into France with the gospel. He believed that the Lord answered yes. Probably he would have been more nearly correct if he had said that he did not hear the Lord say no. At any rate, it seems that Francis, like thousands of Christians before and since, accepted as the voice of God, his own inmost desire. It is comforting to know that the saint of Assisi was as human as we are. He never reached the border. Cardinal Ugolino practically ordered him to remain in Italy lest the enemies of the movement should take advantage of his absence and destroy the cause. And Francis, who by this time had come to accept the fact that there were enemies even within the ranks, conceded and appointed another to take his place in France.

Now that the brothers were witnessing everywhere in "Samaria," Francis began making plans for the next great step in the missionary enterprise—plans that would take the *Fratres Minores* into all nations, teaching, baptizing in the name of the Father, and of the Son, and of the Holy Ghost, while standing on the promise that God would be with them even unto the end of the world.

22

Seed of the Church

Italy enjoyed an open winter in 1218-1219. Snow was seldom seen even on the highest peaks of the Apennines, and temperatures in the valleys of the north and everywhere from Assisi southward hardly reached the freezing point on the coldest days. In January, gardens were being spaded, and fields everywhere were turning prematurely green as all Italy seemed to go singing along the way. Even a leper, asking for alms, was seen to smile pleasantly upon his benefactor as he hummed a simple tune and pursued his lonely existence outside the walls of the city.

Spring came and went. Still there was no noticeable change in the elements until, according to the calendar, summer was well under way. Then waves of intense heat, magnified by a humid, sultry atmosphere, penetrated forest and plain as Italy's fields prepared to yield the greatest crops in history. Mother Nature, it seemed, had never been more generous;

but alas, human nature had seldom been less so.

The fifth Crusade by this time had become another devastating conflict. Among its most inglorious and, at the same time, unnecessary battles was the siege of Damietta. This strategic Egyptian city was fortified with great stone walls from which projected more than a hundred stately towers equipped with crossbows, spears, and javelins; and stored away in its mammoth bins were food supplies to last its citizens and soldiers for more than twenty months if the pope's invading hordes could hold out that long.

The sultan, Malek-el-Kamel, would like to have avoided the long, hard struggle which was bound to cost him dearly, win or lose, and he was ready to compromise. If he could retain Damietta, he would forfeit Jerusalem to the Christians. (Oh blessed hindsight, why must you always be so late appearing?) Had this proposition been accepted by the Pope's legate, Pelagius, a whole new Christendom might have emerged from the Middle Ages. But no! The brave ambitious general was determined to take both Damietta and Jerusalem by aggressive warfare, the only language he understood.

It was to this disparaging theater of war that Francis decided to go, after turning over his responsibility as head of the *Fratres Minores* to his trusted friend, Peter of Catanei. Before he left, he gave what little direction he felt was needed to his men. Brother Elias had already gone to the Holy Land, Brother Giles headed a mission in Tunis, five loyal volunteers were to take the gospel to Morocco, and others were dispatched to many fields. (It should be noted here that, later, following the death of Peter Catanei, Francis appointed Brother Elias minister general of the order.)

Francis chose for his companions several of his most loyal men and, once again, boarded a ship at the port of Ancona. This time the weather was hot and balmy and the seas were calm. Francis was unusually quiet and withdrawn from his fellows as the little sailboat, propelled mostly now by oarsmen, plowed slowly through the tranquil waters.

"What shall be our procedure when we reach the battlefield?" asked one of the men. "Shall we try, Father Francis, to convert the soldiers of the pope's army or those of the Moslems?"

"Perhaps," spoke up another, "it would be better if we could take the message of peace to Pelagius. If we could see a great general in whom the pope places so much confidence accept the gift of peace, we would reach the heart of the problem."

"No," said Francis slowly, "the heart of the problem lies in the Moslem camp. I have decided to go straight to the sultan, Malek-el-Kamel himself; and if the Lord be pleased, we shall lead him to the Cross."

The men looked upon their leader with undisguised amazement.

"I am not asking that any of you accompany me," Francis went on, "that decision must be yours alone, but I must go."

"We will be killed before we get near the sultan!" said one of the brothers in alarm.

"What better death could there be," asked Francis simply, "than to share physically in Christ's own sacrifice and join the martyrs in heaven?"

The men agreed to go along, but when the time came, Francis allowed only one of them to accompany him.

In the meantime, a battle of untold horror raged over Damietta until finally Pelagius and his forces were soundly beaten. Then one day, when all was calm again, Francis approached the legate in his tent.

"I have come to ask permission," he said, "to cross the enemy's lines with one of my friends to seek an audience with the sultan. Evangelism is our aim and faith alone shall be our security."

Pelagius was unable to hide his humorous reaction to the little friar's ridiculous suggestion; either the barefooted preacher in the brown patched tunic was the world's greatest comedian, or he was stark mad. The legate threw back his head and laughed so heartily that his whole body shook with mirth, until a coughing spell nearly made him strangle. Then, gaining control of himself for a moment, he looked into Francis' serious eyes and exploded again, howling with delight. His puffy countenance flushed rosy red as tears cut furrows down his dusty cheeks. Francis waited for the outburst to pass, then asked the favor one more time.

Pelagius clasped his stubby hands across his midriff and nodded profusely. *"Anything,"* he said, *"anything* as long as you get out of my sight before I explode. Ah-a-a-a-a!" He was off again on another laughing spell as Francis hurried away to make his plans.

The following morning Francis and one of his companions made their way into Moslem territory, singing praises unto God. The first of the sultan's soldiers to see the two intruders would have cut them down like poisonous parasites which they considered them to be, if it had not been for the strange appearance and carefree song of the happy evangelists. Instead, the soldiers surrounded them, demanding that they explain their odd behavior and state their business.

"We want to see the sultan," said Francis firmly. "Our mission is one of peace and of utmost importance."

Now it was the soldiers' turn to laugh with glee, for what better entertainment could be found in that bloodstained desert than a couple of wandering lunatics. And the captain of the guard was aware that the sultan, who had been especially good-natured since his recent victory, was sitting in his tent bored for lack of diversion.

"Go to our great leader," he instructed one of his men. "Ask him what he would have us do with these tramps who sing like troubadours and dare invade our territory."

"The fools must be religious fanatics," said Malek-el-Kamel to the soldiers. "Bring them to me at once. I think I shall play cat and mouse with them before I send them to the axe."

The little game, however, took a most unexpected turn. The sultan realized at once that he was dealing with no ordinary mice but with two extraordinary men. Francis' forthright message of peace had within it something frightfully attractive to the Moslem leader. He knew no arguments with which to refute the simple truths presented so logically by the friar. He called his theologians, but those dignitaries would have no part in the discussion; the chopping block was their one answer to the problem. They withdrew.

Then Francis presented the sultan with a new rule of play, which was to determine at once the winner of their contest for truth.

"Instruct your men to hollow out a pit in the sand and make a roaring furnace in it," he said. "Build a fire so hot that it will burn the eyes of those who look upon it. Then call your most devoted priest. He and I shall enter the holocaust together, asking the living Christ and the dead Mohammed each to protect his own."

"I have no priest who would consent to your suggestion," said Malek-el-Kamel sadly.

"Then," said Francis, "build the fire and I shall enter it alone. If I burn, you may impute it to my sins. But if I come through the raging flames unscathed, I shall have your promise to embrace the Christian faith and accept the gift of peace that was purchased for your soul on Calvary."

The sultan looked upon Francis with profound admiration. "You persuade me, *almost,* to be a Christian," he said simply. "You and your friend may go now. My soldiers shall see you safely to the border. Pray for my unworthy soul." Then scribbling a few words above his signature, he presented Francis with a pass to travel freely throughout the Moslem world.

The two missionaries were strangely quiet as they trudged barefooted through the hot sands on their return to their friends, until Francis was faced with a pointed question by his companion.

"What would you have done, Father," he asked, "if the sultan had agreed to your suggestion and called for a fire?"

"I must admit," said Francis, "that I didn't think he would take me up on my proposition, but I had no way of knowing, for the Moslems are often fanatically devout. If he had agreed to either of my suggestions, you may be sure that I would have gone into the furnace with the same lack of resistance that Christ approached the Cross. What less could I have done?"

"What do you think would have happened, Father?" the other asked. "Would the Lord have protected you as He did the Hebrew children in Babylon?"

"I don't know," said Francis thoughtfully. "He would have done the thing that would have brought Him the greater glory."

(That, no doubt, was exactly what He did. It seems too bad, of course, that Francis failed to see the sultan converted, but this one missionary journey may have been among the most significant accomplishments of his dedicated life, for the penetrating of hostile nations with the gospel became forever a living reality.)

Francis' health was breaking, his eyes pained him severely, and his limbs sometimes buckled beneath his weight. He spent most of his time alone in prayer, lying on a hard improvised cot. The autumn and winter months dragged on. Then, in the spring of 1220, his strength returned for a season.

In early June, he and his men took a boat to Acre, an important Palestinian seaport and capital of the kingdom of Jerusalem.

Brother Elias had done good work there. A strong community of *Fratres Minores* was well established, and, for the most part, adhered well to the Primitive Rule.

Francis had been long possessed with two desires. The first—never realized—was to visit France, but the other was being accomplished now in this trip to the Holy Land—to walk where Jesus walked.

Brother Elias staged an elaborate welcome for the leader and his party; anything Elias promoted was certainly to have a magnificent touch. Someday, if he had his way, the whole Franciscan Order would move up from their poverty to outshine in elegance all other orders of the church. Francis, however, remained a trusting soul, and refused steadfastly to believe anything derogatory of Elias. This, some of the brothers said, was the reason he was able to maintain the firm allegiance of the ambitious friar. But there is little doubt that Elias loved and respected Francis with deep devotion, even though he disagreed secretly with his philosophy. Whatever reforms he had in mind he was determined to hold in abeyance until Francis' failing health removed him from the earthly scene. But back in Italy there were other Franciscans of liberal tendencies who were not as thoughtful of the founder's feelings as was Elias and, even then, were taking advantage of their leader's absence to effect drastic changes in the motive, discipline, and prudentials of the order.

Francis' health broke again about a month before he received this discouraging news. "I know how Jesus felt,"

166

he told the brothers in Jerusalem, "when He fell beneath the burden of the Cross. I, too, have fallen; the cross is heavier now than I can bear. But I count my afflictions blessed, for to be counted worthy to share His sufferings is joy unspeakable."

"Your eyes seem terribly affected, Father," said Elias one morning a few weeks later. "Would you like to talk about it?"

"I have been thanking God for allowing me the privilege of having seen the beauty of His wonderful creation," mused Francis. "For three days now I have seen only the light of Brother Sun, but what greater blessing is there than the light? When I have rested, perhaps my eyes shall look upon the hills and trees again. Until then, the songs of my sisters, the birds, will be more beautiful than I ever knew them in the past."

In the days that followed, Francis' vision came and went while his body weakened, but his lovely tenor voice retained enough of its luster that songs of praise and promise were on his lips continually, and not one word of complaint was known to escape him.

Then came Brother Stephen all the way from Italy with important news for Francis. For months the loyal friar had hounded his leader's trail, and little less than a miracle of heaven led him to the friar's tiny camp outside Jerusalem. When he stood beside the pallet where Francis lay, he wept as he looked upon the gaunt, emaciated body of his dearest friend. He wondered whether Francis had the strength to withstand the shock of the disturbing news he carried.

"You bring me word from home, Brother Stephen?" asked Francis hopefully.

"Yes, Father," said the friar sadly. "I wish only that what I have to say could bring you joy."

"Go on, Stephen," the other answered firmly. "To delay will not improve it, I am sure."

Stephen laid his hand upon Francis' shoulder. "Father," he said, "the five brothers who carried the gospel into Morocco were all beheaded. Brother Sylvester maintains that they went at once to be with all the martyrs of the past."

"Praise be to God!" Francis was speaking with great fervor. "Without the blood of martyrs, there would be no church." And if he had known then that from their labors would come one Anthony of Padua, who eventually would be numbered among the greatest of all Franciscan saints, his joy would have known no bounds. "What other news do you bring, Brother Stephen?" he asked.

The friar proceeded to explain to him the internal troubles that harassed the Lesser Brothers. "Many of the men, however, are remaining loyal to the rule," he said, "and the gospel is being carried to the far corners of the earth. But we fear that your prolonged absence is not good, and your friends want you to return at once, dear Father."

Francis fell to reminiscing. "When I was a boy I owned a beautiful black filly," he said. "One day I sold her in Foligno, and I have never ridden since. But now that my strength is gone, if you can provide a donkey somehow, I will ride again. God will see that I reach the Little Portion one more time."

"Yes, Father," Elias broke in kindly, "we will take a boat to Venice as soon as you are able to travel. There we shall find a farmer who will trade a donkey for our labor, and soon we will be home again."

So it was that on one of the first cool days of autumn the little troup of *Fratres Minores,* dressed in their patched brown tunics—one of them leading a donkey that bore their leader—came singing through the gates of Assisi.

23

Well Done

The state of affairs that Francis found upon his return to the home base could hardly have been more discouraging. His depression became so great that a lesser saint than he might well have been drawn down into its clammy atmosphere. At Bologna, where Bernard di Quintavalle had given his best years to establish a strong chapter of *Fratres Minores,* the brothers had come under the influence of liberal leadership and were living in rich, plush quarters near the university. When news of this innovation into the order that openly defied the Primitive Rule reached Francis, he asked to be taken to Bologna without delay. It was a dreary, rainy day when the trip was undertaken. with Francis still suffering from the effects of his long, hazardous journey. Every muscle of his body seemed to ache; and his eyes, burning in their sockets, refused to function. Of all men, he was indeed most miserable.

The ambitious friar, who had promoted the radical changes in the order, was brought before the leader to look with scorn upon the gaunt, emaciated figure—a shadow of the former Francis, son of Pietro di Bernardone.

The little evangelist's scraggly hair and sparse beard accentuated his oval face which was marred now with furrows that cut deeply into the benign countenance, adding, in appearance, decades to his forty years. The brother who virtually had been reprimanded severely anticipated no serious problem. After all, his idealistic leader was blind and ill, bent and nearly broken. (Maybe the money changers in the temple were unable also to imagine the Prince of Peace capable of wielding a cat-o'-nine-tails, scattering their ill-gotten gains and terminating their lucrative enterprises.) In any event, Francis had reached the breaking point. Never since his marriage to Lady Poverty had he allowed himself the questionable pleasure of unrestrained response to any outside stimulus. But this one time he came out of his monastic shell with all the vigor of a caged leopard that had suddenly found its freedom. What wouldn't we give for a tape recording of the fiery lecture that exploded literally from the lips of the Saint of Assisi, cutting the startled heretic to the core, causing him to swallow all his cynicism, pride, and prejudice in one great gulp!

In the days that followed, Francis' mental anguish superceded his physical distresses. The deterioration of the order which he had so painfully established seemed more than he could bear, and his angry outburst at Bologna condemned him in spirit until he believed that he had failed in every endeavor of his life. He was totally blind now; darkness, literally and figuratively, enveloped him completely—body, soul, and spirit.

So it came about that, in his anguish, he asked the brothers to take him to Mount La Verna where he might dwell alone with the Man of Sorrows—the One who had walked the roads of earth to experience every temptation and disappointment that is known to man, but who yielded never to the pressures of the world. And it was there that Francis recalled how, years before, in one of their counseling sessions, the old priest of San Damiano had prepared him for such a day as this.

"Revival comes and goes," old Peter had said. "It must necessarily be so; otherwise, one such awakening is all the church would ever need. But evangelism is continuing—a chain which sometimes wears as thin as thread but never breaks, holding the militant church together between the great awakenings. One cannot live without the other."

Francis, in his disappointment, clung desperately to these words which he had nearly forgotten. He was at least vaguely cognizant that the deep spiritual experience with which the Lord had decreed that he should seed the church would flow like tiny rivulets, forever, from the reservoirs of faith. This seeding would save the church of Jesus Christ in days when leanness once again would overtake it. His joy, no doubt, would have returned at once if he could have known that centuries later, a girl in France whose zeal would proclaim her a heretic and cost her her life would bear testimony to the world that a humble Franciscan friar had taught her the way of faith and led her to the Cross. She would be known to all Christendom as Madam Guyan.

So finally it was alone on Mount La Verna that Francis found again the peace that passes understanding. He regained complete victory over the world, the flesh, and the devil to dwell in ecstasy in the Divine Presence knowing that he had succeeded in his commission to *repair His house.* Some of the brothers claimed to have seen Christ's nail prints in Francis' hands and feet—proclaiming the miracle of the stigmata—when later he was carried back to San Damiano where, for seven weeks in the summer of 1225, Sister Clare cared for him through the most precious of his final days. Francis' suffering was inconceivable, but he never failed to sing as his lovely tenor voice grew weaker. Blind and bent but never broken, he composed his "Canticle to the Sun," which has been described as the most beautiful spiritual poetry since the gospels.

> Most High, Almighty, good Lord,
> Thine be the praise, the glory, the honor,
> And all blessing.

To Thee, alone, Most High, are they due,
And no man is worthy
To speak Thy Name.

Praise to Thee, my Lord, for all Thy creatures,
Above all, Brother Sun
Who brings us the day and lends us his light.

Lovely is he, radiant with great splendor,
And speaks to us of Thee,
O Most High.

Praise to Thee, my Lord, for Sister Moon and the stars
Which Thou hast set in the heavens,
Clear, precious, and fair.

Praise to Thee, my Lord, for Brother Wind,
For air and cloud, for calm and all weather,
By which Thou supportest life in all Thy creatures.

Praise to Thee, my Lord, for Sister Water,
Who is so useful and humble,
Precious and pure.

Praise to Thee, my Lord, for Brother Fire,
By whom Thou lightest the night;
He is lovely and pleasant, mighty and strong.

Praise to Thee, my Lord, for our Sister Mother Earth
Who sustains and directs us,
And brings forth varied fruits, and colored flowers, and plants.

Praise to Thee, my Lord, for those who pardon one another
For love of Thee and endure
Sickness and tribulation.
Blessed are they who shall endure it in peace,
For they shall be crowned by Thee,
O Most High.

For reasons hard to understand today, the suffering saint
was carried by his friends from place to place, finally to the
Little Portion and Saint Mary's of the Angels. He was
supremely happy in his devastating pain which he bore

172

with love for Christ and the world, as he awaited his release from the vale of sorrows. He asked to be taken from his crude bed that he might lie once more on the hard, cool bosom of Mother Earth. Then he called the brothers around him to sing his "Canticle to the Sun." When the song was finished, he added a final stanza, his "Canticle to Sister Death":

Praise to Thee, my Lord, for our Sister Bodily Death
From whom no man living may escape;
Woe to those who die in mortal sin.

Blessed are they who are found in Thy most holy will,
For the second death cannot harm them.

Praise and bless my Lord,
Thank Him and serve Him
With great humility.

The purest, sweetest soul since Christ Himself was going home. The brothers in their plain brown tunics of sackcloth wept without restraint as they looked upon their leader whose smile became as heavenly as the billowy clouds that hung that day above the vale of Umbria. Then Francis of Assisi calmly breathed his last to be welcomed into paradise by Christ Himself, who must have said, "Well done, My good and faithful servant; *you repaired My house.*"